BEST IN SNOW

ALSO BY DAVID ROSENFELT

BEST IN SNOW

David Rosenfelt

MINOTAUR BOOKS
NEW YORK

First published in the United States by Minotaur Books, an imprint of St. Martin's Publishing Group

BEST IN SNOW. Copyright © 2021 by Tara Productions, Inc. All rights reserved. Printed in the United States of America. For information, address St. Martin's Publishing Group, 120 Broadway, New York, NY 10271.

www.minotaurbooks.com

Library of Congress Cataloging-in-Publication Data

Names: Rosenfelt, David, author.
Title: Best in snow / David Rosenfelt.
Description: First Edition. | New York : Minotaur Books, 2021.
Identifiers: LCCN 2021026593 | ISBN 9781250257178 (hardcover) | ISBN 9781250836564 (Canadian edition) | ISBN 9781250257161 (ebook)
Subjects: GSAFD: Mystery fiction.
Classification: LCC PS3618.O838 B47 2021 | DDC 813/.6—dc23
LC record available at https://lccn.loc.gov/2021026593

Our books may be purchased in bulk for promotional, educational, or business use. Please contact your local bookseller or the Macmillan Corporate and Premium Sales Department at 1-800-221-7945, extension 5442, or by email at MacmillanSpecialMarkets@macmillan.com.

First U.S. Edition: 2021
First Canadian Edition: 2021

10 9 8 7 6 5 4 3 2 1

This book is dedicated to Ron Ranes.
Intelligence. Humor. Courage. Friendship.
The whole package.

BEST IN SNOW

The night turned out to be significantly worse than Alex Oliva expected.

He'd dressed in a suit and tie for one of the seemingly never-ending series of charity dinners he was forced to attend. This one was not going to be as bad as most because he wasn't being called on to give a speech.

All he had to lend to the event was his presence and his willingness to shake a lot of hands, but his seat on the dais unfortunately meant that there would be no quick getaway. So he was resigned to a night of smiling, working the room, and, he hoped, being out of there by ten o'clock. It would be relatively miserable but was part of the process, and he was used to it.

None of that happened. Alex left his house through the back door and was shot in the back as he reached the garage. The bullet was perfectly placed, passing through his heart as it went through his body.

If Alex felt any surprise or pain, it was momentary. His killer picked up his body and carried it off, to be left at a place of his choosing. The entire operation took less than two minutes.

But one thing was for sure . . . there would be an empty seat on the dais.

Edna is getting married! Edna is getting married!

I don't want to seem too gleeful about this, so let me rephrase it.

Edna is getting married . . . hmmm, that's nice.

First, a little background on Edna and me. I'm a defense attorney, and I have employed Edna for more than twenty years. She has been my self-described secretary, executive assistant, and office manager. Her job hasn't changed, but the titles she has given herself have evolved along with workplace conventions.

Most significantly, her job has remained consistent in one specific aspect: she does absolutely no work. She avoids it like the plague, though until recently she was willing to make the effort to cash her checks. She finally set up direct deposit, just to make the whole thing less exhausting.

Of course, if someone is intent on not working, I'm a pretty good lawyer to not work for. I am in semi-retirement due to significant wealth and significant laziness. I have to be dragged kicking and screaming into a case. Once I take on a client, it's Edna who does the kicking and screaming.

The guy she is marrying is David Divine, who I've met tonight for the first time. Edna has brought him over to our place for coffee; she said that it was important to her that he meet me and my wife, Laurie Collins. Our son, Ricky, is not home tonight; he has a sleepover at his friend Will Rubenstein's house. They seem to have sleepovers pretty much every nonschool night. Half the time Will's family is the host, as they are tonight, and the other half we get the honor.

David owns twelve Taco Bell restaurants spread throughout the Northeast, though he's just mentioned that he's planning to sell them and retire. I would estimate that he and Edna are both in their mid-to-late sixties, and David says that they want to travel a lot . . . to "see the world."

My assumption, though it hasn't been mentioned, is that Edna is going to retire as well. She'll have no financial reason to work, and it's not like she loves her job. It's not even like she does her job.

It's been a relatively pleasant evening so far, though it's becoming a long one. I'm starting on my fourth cup of coffee, and I don't particularly like the stuff. Laurie and I have been making eye contact for about twenty minutes. My eyes have been saying, *When are they going to leave?* Her eyes have responded with *Be nice, Andy.* My eyes haven't come up with a good comeback to that.

Making matters worse is the insufferable Christmas music that has been on in the house for the entire evening. We're just approaching Thanksgiving, but that is well within the four-month marathon that Laurie considers Christmas. It is making me wish I took cyanide in my coffee.

Our dogs are starting to stir; since they haven't had any coffee, they've been asleep this whole time. But their awakening can give me an out.

We have three dogs. Tara is the greatest golden retriever

the world has ever known, Sebastian is the laziest basset hound on the planet, and Hunter, the pug, is the newcomer in the group and still feeling his way. For now he's content to emulate and idolize Tara, which makes him one smart pug.

"Looks like they are ready for their nighttime walk," I say. "I always walk them just before bed."

"Where do you take them?" David asks.

"Eastside Park."

"I'd love to go along."

"Super," I lie. Eastside Park is fairly close by; I should have said Central Park or Yellowstone National. Maybe David would have been less anxious to make the trek.

So we set out; I hold the leashes for Tara and Hunter, while he takes Sebastian's. It's cold out, and we had a somewhat unseasonable nine-inch snowfall last night, which makes it feel like the dead of winter.

I'm going to shorten our normal walk, both because of the weather and because as long as we are out, David and Edna are obviously not going home. We head for Eastside Park, but rather than go deep into the park, we'll just go a short way in and then turn around.

The sidewalks are well shoveled, which makes the walk easy, although Tara likes to walk along the side, in the snow. Hunter, ever loyal to his friend, does the same, and although the depth of the snow makes it hard for him, he soldiers on. Sebastian characteristically takes the easier path; if there were a moving walkway, or an Uber, Sebastian would take one of them.

We haven't talked too much so far, just about the weather

and yesterday's snowfall. I finally decide to confront the elephant in the park.

"So I guess Edna will be retiring? I'm really going to miss her."

"Retire?" He laughs. "Not a chance. She loves her job; what would she do every day?"

"I've wondered that myself. I just assumed she'd be leaving, since you both said how much you want to travel and see the world."

He nods. "And we do; in fact, we've already booked a Baltic cruise. Edna said that she has months of vacation time accrued. Said she hasn't taken a vacation in years."

I'm at a loss for words; an unusual occurrence for me. Finally I come up with a few. "Yeah, she's a workaholic, that Edna. We try to get her to take it easy, but she won't hear of it."

The road leading into the park is plowed pretty well, and we walk for about a hundred yards. As we're about to turn around, Tara gets excited about something. This is not an unusual occurrence; it happens every time she spots a squirrel, and the park is filled with squirrels.

Because it's late and no one else is around, I drop the leash so she can chase the squirrel, even though I haven't actually seen it. I have no concern that she will catch it; they haven't invented the squirrel that Tara could catch.

Hunter also wants to run off after her, but I hold on to his leash. We haven't had him that long, and I don't fully trust him to come back.

In Tara I trust.

I'm surprised to see that Tara runs about thirty feet into

the deep snow and stops. She starts digging in the snow; I sure as hell hope no wounded squirrel is lying there. I hand Hunter's leash to David and run through the snow to investigate.

There's a decent amount of moonlight, but I still can't see what Tara must see, or more likely smell.

David comes up behind me with the two dogs. "What did she find?"

"I'm not sure."

David takes out his phone and activates its flashlight. As he does, Tara pulls back, almost as if she is surprised by her own discovery.

David shines the flashlight on the hole Tara has dug, and what it reveals leaves us all stunned. It even causes David to let out a small scream.

It's a human hand.

M y first call is to Pete Stanton.

Pete, the captain in charge of Paterson PD Homicide, is also a close friend, a sports-watching and beer-drinking buddy. I call him rather than 911 because I know from experience that David and I are going to be stuck here for a long time.

If I call 911, as I'm sure I'm supposed to, they'll send out officers, who will then just turn around and call Homicide. This skips that step.

So far all I've seen is the hand sticking out of the snow, so I have no insight as to what the hell is going on. But even though I called Pete, it seems more likely than not that it is not a murder. My guess would be someone walking in the park had a heart attack and collapsed and got snowed on.

My second call is to Laurie, and she and Edna are going to come right over and get the dogs. Even in a best case, David and I are going to be here for a good while, giving our statements and describing how we found the body. Of course, that is assuming the hand is attached to a body.

The first to arrive are three police cars, each containing two officers. David and I and the dogs have moved well back from the scene, so as not to contaminate any possible evidence. I tell the officers where the discovery was made. Two of them go over there, and the others stay with us, a possible sign of lack of trust.

Laurie and Edna arrive, which increases the trust, since Laurie knows two of the cops from back in the days when she was on the force. After talking to them for a few minutes, she and Edna take the dogs and head home.

Nobody is telling us anything, but the place is certainly starting to look like a crime scene. Other cops arrive, including some who I recognize as homicide detectives. Forensics is also there, doing what forensics does, and a coroner's van shows up as well.

About fifteen minutes later Pete arrives, followed by another five squad cars. They are treating this as a major event; this isn't feeling like a heart attack victim who got snowed on.

Pete consults with his detectives, then comes over to me. "You seem to attract dead bodies," he says, a reference to the number of murder cases I've handled. As I said, Pete and I are close friends, but I can't remember the last nice thing we said to each other.

"It's not me. People tend to commit murders in Paterson because they know you'll never catch them. You can't blame them; you're a walking 'stay out of jail free' card."

He ignores that. "So you two were just out for a stroll in the snow?"

"We were walking the dogs."

He nods. "That I believe."

"Tara started digging where the body was. So if you see paw prints, don't think of it as a clue and start arresting golden retrievers."

"Officers will get your statements and then you can leave."

"Is it a murder?"

He hesitates, then nods. "Unless he accidentally shot himself in the back."

"Who's the victim?"

"I don't think I'm going to share that with you at this point. Did Tara dig up any clues I should be aware of?"

"No, but if you want to borrow her for a few days, you can. She'd have a better chance of solving this than you would."

"Great talking to you."

I'm not quite ready to let Pete go. "Was the guy killed here? Because I didn't see much blood."

"When we finish the investigation, you'll be the first person we brief on it. Now, any other questions? Because my only real goal here is to satisfy your curiosity."

"No, you can go play detective."

We give our statements and head home. David seems shaken by what has transpired. "Except for my father, that's the first dead body I've ever seen."

"All you saw was the hand."

"That was plenty."

We get home and it's another half hour and two cups of coffee before they finally leave. It is a night that they will not soon forget. I won't either.

Laurie, ex-cop and investigator that she is, asks me a bunch of questions about the murder, few of which I can answer.

When we're getting into bed, Laurie says, "By the way, Edna told me that she is going to continue to work."

"Continue?"

"You know what I mean."

"Unfortunately I do."

"But she's going to travel. Can she do that and fulfill her responsibilities?

"Sure. She has direct deposit."

Did I wake you?" the voice on the phone asks.

It sounds like Vince Sanders, but the ringing phone did, in fact, wake me, so I'm not thinking too clearly. I didn't sleep well, possibly because I had a bathtub-ful of coffee last night.

I look at the clock, see that it's six thirty, and say, "Vince?"

"No, it's LeBron James. Of course it's Vince."

"Then the answer to your question is yes, you woke me. What the hell is going on?" I look over and see that Laurie is not in bed. That is explained by the whirring sound coming from the exercise room; she is on the bike, pedaling furiously to nowhere. I can also hear the television; Laurie watches the news in the morning while she rides.

"A body was found in Eastside Park last night," he says.

"I have firsthand knowledge of that. I discovered it; or, more accurately, Tara did."

"You're bullshitting me."

Vince is the editor of our local newspaper, so I'm not surprised he would already be aware of last night's events. What I'm not clear on is why he's sharing the news with me at six thirty in the morning. Having said that, I can tell from his voice that he is upset.

"Vince, I am not bullshitting you. I'm not even sure why I'm talking to you."

"What were you doing in the park at night?"

"What am I, a suspect? I told you, we were walking the dogs."

"What is it with you and dogs?"

Vince has never quite understood the human-canine connection. "Vince, can you get to the point here? I am still entertaining the possibility of going back to sleep."

"Do you know who the dead guy is?"

"I do not; all I saw was his hand, and I didn't recognize it."

"Alex Oliva."

"Mayor Alex Oliva?"

"One and the same."

"Tara dug up the mayor of Paterson?"

"She did."

"This is fascinating news, Vince. But if you didn't know that Tara and I dug up the body, why are you calling me at this hour of the morning to make the identification?"

"I can't find Bobby Nash."

That clears it up a little, but not all the way. Bobby Nash is a young reporter who used to work for Vince. He ran a negative story about the mayor that ultimately cost Bobby his job when it turned out to be false. I know that Vince really liked Bobby and was upset when he had to let him go.

What I don't understand is why Vince is looking for Bobby and why he has felt the need to involve me. "Why are you trying to find him?"

"Because the police are looking for him."

"Is he a suspect?"

"They won't say. Even Pete won't tell me, do you believe that?"

Pete Stanton, Vince, and I share a regular table at Charlie's Sports Bar. We're friends in that we spend a lot of time watching sports, drinking beer, and insulting one another without feeling insulted.

"I believe it. The mayor has been killed; it's red alert time in city government. The pressure will be on Pete like it's never been on him before. He can handle it, but I'm sure he doesn't want you quoting him in the paper."

"It's not Pete I'm worried about; it's Bobby."

"You think he's running away?"

"I don't know."

"If you're looking for my advice, keep trying to find him and make him available to the police. Running would only show consciousness of guilt. By the way, do you think he could have done it?"

"No chance."

"Good."

"Will you help him?" It's hard for me to hear Vince because there is the simultaneous crashing sound of my heart hitting the floor.

"Help him how?"

"If they question him, or even arrest him, he's going to need a lawyer."

"I can recommend someone really good."

"Not as good as you. Come on, Andy, you owe me one."

"I owe you one? From when?" One major favor has been done in our relationship, a long time ago, and it was done by me for Vince.

"Let me put it another way. If you ever needed me, I

would be there for you, and then you would owe me one. It's not my fault you've never needed me. You have only yourself to blame."

That has a certain twisted logic to it, and more than a grain of truth. As irascible and obnoxious as Vince can be, there is no question I could count on him if I had to.

"Vince, let's let it play out. Okay? I'll do what I can when the time comes, but you know I don't want to take on clients."

"This isn't a client. He's my friend."

"Let's see where it goes." I'm making the least commitment I can in the moment, leaving me leeway to bob and weave later on.

Just then Laurie comes into the room, an intense look on her face.

"Hold on a second, Vince." I turn to Laurie. "What's going on?"

"It's on the news . . . that body you found was the mayor."

"I know. Vince just told me."

"Did he also tell you that they arrested Bobby Nash?"

I put the phone back to my ear. "Vince, remember I said we should let it play out?"

"Yeah . . . so?"

"So it just played out."

There is nothing defense attorneys like to talk about more than a "rush to judgment."

It is a club we use against police and prosecutors, and that it rarely works does not deter us any. No matter how long an investigation takes, we claim it should have taken longer, and that the police were guilty of that awful rush to judgment in arresting our innocent client.

The logic behind it is compelling, and rests not on what the police did, but rather on what they didn't do. An arrest doesn't stop an investigation in its tracks, but it changes the focus and direction. From then on, the goal is to get more evidence against the charged person, to make the case stronger.

Obviously, this is at the expense of looking for other possible perpetrators. Once the police think they have the guilty party, then hunting for the guilty party seems a bit silly. So by claiming a rush to judgment, we are bemoaning that the police have stopped looking for the real killer.

I know nothing about the murder of Mayor Alex Oliva, even though Tara and I set the investigation into motion. But it would be hard to imagine a faster rush to judgment: the arrest came less than eight hours after Tara started digging in the snow.

That's not to say that the police are wrong, that they have the wrong man. Ironically, the speed might well indicate that the opposite is true. Knowing that they could be criticized for moving too quickly, they would most likely not have done so if they were not extremely confident in their evidence.

I would like to be observing this from afar, very far afar. But I can't because Vince played the friendship card on me. So I've agreed to meet and talk to Bobby Nash this afternoon, after he's settled in the jail. I've made no commitment about representation, but I know that's what Vince is angling for.

I hate friendship. Friendship is for suckers.

I know something about the episode that got Bobby Nash fired, but not as much as I'm going to need to know. The solution to that, like the solution to every problem known to humankind, is Google. So I spent an hour in Google-land this morning.

Bobby authored a story accusing Mayor Oliva of steering a large hospital-construction project to a company run by a prominent northern–New Jersey businessman, Richard Minchner. The mayor did so, according to Bobby, in return for a million-dollar contribution to a PAC set up to support Oliva's expected run for governor.

The published story only quoted an anonymous source. This would ordinarily not have been enough except that Bobby had copies of three canceled checks from one of Minchner's companies, adding up to the total of a million dollars.

The mayor and Minchner both went nuts, claiming that the story was bogus. Few people believed them, until Minchner authorized the bank to make his records public.

The checks, it turned out, were elaborate fakes that had never been written at all. They had the correct account number and appeared legitimate, but they were not.

Even though Vince didn't talk about it, the incident was devastating to Vince. Lawsuits were threatened and quickly filed, and my guess is that only Vince's reputation and that he is pretty much an institution in local journalism saved his own job.

But he was forced to let Bobby go; that was a no-brainer. It was, along with a retraction and an apology, the condition under which the lawsuits were dropped. Mayor Oliva then made political hay out of the incident by claiming the media was against him because he was bucking the establishment. It enhanced his reputation, rather than destroying it.

The whole thing was particularly upsetting to Vince because Bobby was Vince's protégé, and Vince seemed to genuinely like him. That placed Bobby in select company, alongside beer, hamburgers, and the New York Mets as the only things that Vince cared deeply about.

I'm about to call the jail to confirm that I can see Bobby if I come down there when Vince calls again: "He's in the hospital."

"Who? Bobby? Did he resist arrest?"

"He was in a car accident sometime during the night. That's how the police found him."

"A car accident? What the hell is going on, Vince?"

"I don't know; that's all I was able to find out. I figured maybe you could learn more, since you're his lawyer."

"Vince, I never said I would be his lawyer."

"So fake it. But tell them you're his lawyer and see what you can find out."

"Did you ask Pete?"

"Pete won't tell me anything."

"I'll try him and get back to you."

I hang up and call Pete. He answers with "Vince tell you to call?"

"He did."

"He's driving me crazy. What is it with him and this kid?"

"He's the kid's mentor. Vince's fatherly instinct is coming out."

"Vince doesn't have a fatherly instinct. He doesn't even have a human instinct. But I'll tell you the same thing I told him, which is nothing."

"Here's the thing, Pete. At least for now, I'm Bobby Nash's attorney."

"You've got to be kidding."

"I wish I was. It's a short-term favor for Vince. But because of that, I'm entitled to learn what's going on."

"Not from me."

"I understand that. But one way or the other I am going to find out, so you would be doing me a big favor by not making me go through the hassle."

He thinks about this for a few moments, no doubt weighing the positives and negatives. "As I recall, you told me I had no chance of catching the killer. You said that murders are committed in Paterson because they know I won't solve them. I believe I'm quoting you accurately."

"I was wrong, Pete. You are one of the finest law enforcement officers of your generation. You make Eliot Ness look like T. S. Eliot."

"What does T. S. stand for?"

"Tough Shit. Tough Shit Eliot. Now will you tell me what's going on?"

"Can I assume you will continue to pay the tab for the burgers and beer at Charlie's for as long as we both shall live?"

"For all of eternity. And that includes the french fries."

"Okay, but there's a lot I can't tell you. What do you want to know?"

"Tell me about the car accident."

"He drove his car off the road and down into a deep ditch; he was knocked unconscious. A couple of broken bones, cracked ribs, and a pretty bad concussion. He'll pull through, but he'll probably wish he didn't."

"When did this happen?"

"About two hours after the estimated time of Oliva's death, if you're scoring at home."

"And he's been in the hospital all this time?"

"You got it. Toxicology should be back anytime."

"You suspect drugs?"

"Strongly."

"What ties him to the murder?"

"That I can't tell you, but it's a lock."

"I've heard that before."

"They found blood in the car."

"He was in an accident. I assume he bled."

"Really? Was he sitting in the trunk when the crash happened?"

"The blood was in the trunk?"

I can almost see Pete smiling through the phone. "Let's see you explain that away, counselor."

Here's how I hope my conversation with Bobby Nash will go:

> BOBBY: "What are you doing here?"
> ME: "Vince asked me to represent you."
> BOBBY: "I'm sorry . . . this is awkward, but my cousin
> Harold is a lawyer, and he's going to handle my case.
> You should enjoy your retirement; I'm sticking with
> Harold."

I don't care if it goes exactly like that; I can be flexible. For instance, I don't care if Bobby's lawyer cousin is named Harold. The name can be Ralph or Guido or Muriel. The net result would be the same.

I'm waiting to be brought into Bobby's hospital room. He's apparently out of danger, but pretty banged up. I haven't told Vince about my conversation with Pete; I decided I'd hear Bobby's side of it first. Then maybe I can claim attorney-client privilege and not talk to Vince at all.

"Carpenter?"

I look up and see a uniformed officer who has just opened the door to the waiting room.

"That's me."

"Let's go."

We walk down the hospital corridor. I can tell where we're going because I see another cop sitting in a chair outside a room. When we get there, the second cop says, "You've got twenty minutes."

I shake my head. "Here's how this works. I'm his lawyer, so I've got as long as I want. I might even decide to sleep over if I can borrow some pajamas. If you have an issue with that, you can vent your feelings to a judge tomorrow morning."

I don't wait for an answer; I just open the door and go into Bobby's room. I've met him a couple of times, but he looked a hell of a lot different then. For one thing, he didn't look like he'd been through a meat grinder.

He looks up at me for a few moments, as if trying to figure out who I am. I'm pretty sure I'm right about that because finally he asks me in a weak voice, "Who are you?"

"Andy Carpenter. I'm a lawyer. Vince asked me to come talk to you."

He thinks for a moment, then a light goes on in his eyes, although it's dim. "Right. Andy Carpenter. I remember you."

"Okay. We're making progress. How are you feeling?"

"Pretty bad; they tell me I have a concussion, a bunch of broken bones, and four cracked ribs. It would hurt to laugh if I had something to laugh about."

"I understand."

"What is going on? How did I get here? What happened to me? Why do I have this?"

To demonstrate what "this" is, he holds up his right hand, showing me that it is cuffed to the bed. His left leg is secured to the bed as well.

"They haven't told you anything?"

"Just that I'm under arrest; they wouldn't say what for. I think they read me my rights, but I was pretty foggy at the time."

"You've been charged with murdering Mayor Alex Oliva."

"What? Come on. . . ."

The look of shock on his face seems real, but more important, it's the first sign of life I've seen out of him.

"It's true, Bobby. Believe me, I wouldn't make that up. Do you know how you got hurt?"

"No. That was my next question. But murder? Is this a bad dream? Am I going to wake up from this?"

"No, you're as awake as you're going to get. You were in a car accident; you went off the road and down into some kind of deep ditch, or ravine."

"This cannot be real."

"You don't remember any of this?"

"No."

"What's the last thing you remember?"

He pauses to think, and the thinking goes on for a solid minute. In thinking terms, that's a long time. Then, "I was at the Crow's Nest."

"What is that?"

"It's a bar . . . off Route Eighty. I think it's in Hackensack, or Hasbrouck Heights."

"Do you remember leaving there?"

Another pause, though not quite as long. "No. I don't think so."

"Have you ever taken drugs, Bobby?"

He holds up his arm, with has an IV in it, with liquid dripping down from a bag. "Is that what this is?"

"No, I mean recreational drugs."

A pause, then, "No. Never. I smoked marijuana a couple of times in high school, but it didn't really affect me."

"You're sure?"

"What? Yes. Look, I'm sorry, but I'm having trouble focusing on what you're saying."

Just then a nurse comes in and looks up in surprise when she sees that I am here. "It's time for Mr. Nash to get his meds and have his vital signs checked. You'll have to wait outside until I'm finished."

She says it in that nice but insistent way nurses have. She's a lot tougher than that cop sitting outside the door. I'm a big fan of nurses; along with volunteer firefighters, they are probably our two highest life-forms.

"That's okay, I'm going anyway." I take out my card and put it on the table next to him. "Bobby, we'll talk again soon, but if you need me before then, here's my number."

"Thank you. I'll try and remember more."

"For now, just take it easy. If it's going to come to you, it will come to you. And don't talk to anyone else about your situation."

As I'm leaving, I hear him asking no one in particular, "Mayor Oliva?"

His version is that he has no recollection of anything and had no idea why he was even in custody."

"I take it you don't believe him?" Laurie asks.

"I don't believe or disbelieve him. I don't have a clue what is going on or what happened. One thing I do know is that blood was found in the trunk of his car."

"Was it the mayor's blood?"

"I don't know. But they certainly couldn't have conducted tests on it by the time they made the arrest. Which means they had other reasons to believe he was connected to the murder."

"Did you learn any more about the drugs in his system?"

"He denies he has taken any. I haven't seen the toxicology yet; I only know what Pete told me."

"Have you talked to Vince?"

"Not yet. He's called me three times; I dread it, but I have to call him back."

The doorbell rings, sending Tara, Sebastian, and Hunter into a barking frenzy. Laurie goes to get it and comes back with Vince, which doesn't exactly shock me.

"Hi, Vince."

"I called you three times."

"I was about to call you back. I was just telling Laurie how much I was looking forward to our conversation."

"Yeah, right. Bring me up to date."

I look over at Laurie and she silently nods, telling me that she thinks I should tell Vince what I know, little as it is.

"Vince, can I get you something?" she asks.

"You have Diet Coke?"

She nods. "Yes."

"Then give it to Andy, so he keeps a clear head. I'll take three beers."

"Three?"

"I'm saving you two trips."

Laurie heads off to get the drinks, and I wait for her to get back before I answer Vince's questions. "Let's start with Bobby," I say. "Ordinarily I would not be able to share anything with you without his permission because of attorney-client privilege. But in this case I can, because he had basically nothing to say."

"What does that mean?"

"He doesn't remember anything about the night in question, including how he crashed his car. He said he was not even aware of why he was under arrest."

"Is that because of the concussion?"

"I have no idea what happened to his memory. Hopefully it will come back and he will be able to explain everything."

"What do you mean 'explain everything'? What is there to explain? Did you talk to Pete? The son of a bitch won't tell me anything."

I nod. "I talked to him. He told me not to share anything with you."

"But you will, right?"

"Of course, but you're not going to like it. They found blood in the trunk of Bobby's car."

"So?" Vince challenges.

"So do you have blood in the trunk of your car?"

He ignores that. "What else did he say?"

"He thinks Bobby had been taking drugs."

"No chance. What else?"

"That's basically it. What's more important is what he didn't say. If they made the arrest that quickly, they must have other evidence that they consider a sure thing. He wouldn't discuss it with me."

"There is no way Bobby did this. You have to help him, Andy."

"Tell us about your relationship with him, Vince," Laurie says, having come back into the room with the drinks. Her tone surprises me; she's using her no-nonsense voice. I recognize it from when she tells me not to put off taking out the garbage because it's overflowing.

She continues, "Vince, you're asking Andy to do a lot here; you know that. So let's have it all; no bullshit." Laurie could not accurately be described as a delicate flower.

"I like the kid," Vince says.

"Vince . . ." Laurie can admonish someone just be saying their name. It's a trait I have long admired.

"Okay. There's more than that; but I do like him. I hired him; first he worked as my assistant before he moved up to doing actual reporting. He reminded me of me starting out."

"Just what we need," I say. "Two Vinces."

Vince ignores that, as he should. "When he came to me

with the story about the mayor, I talked him through it. I questioned him, I helped him, I almost wrote the damn thing for him. But most of all, I approved it. I gave him the green light; it's what editors do."

"So?"

"So it blew up in his face, which means it blew up in my face."

"You must have had good reason to approve the story," Laurie says.

Vince nods. "It seemed like it at the time. He had the copies of the canceled checks and he said he had a woman on the inside at the mayor's reelection committee who supplied them and told him what was going on. Her name is Theresa Minardo, but she insisted on staying anonymous."

"And she hung Bobby out to dry?" I ask.

"She did. When the checks were shown to be fake, she denied everything. Said she never saw the checks and Bobby was lying about her involvement. She's the villain of the piece. Someone must have used her to get the mayor, but she left herself an out. There was no way for Bobby to prove that she was the source."

"So he never had a prayer."

"Right. So what happened?" Vince asks. "To me, very little . . . almost nothing. To him, he lost his job and career. And I had to be the one to fire him. Worst day of my life."

"Why did you do it?"

"Couple of reasons, but the main one is because I was a weak piece of shit. The other reason is that he was gone anyway; whether I did it or not, whether I got fired or not, he was gone. And if we were both fired, I couldn't have helped him."

"You've been helping him?" I ask.

He nods. "Yeah. I've been hiring him for freelance stuff. He's been writing under a pseudonym. And I got some friends at other papers to do the same. Nothing big, just enough to let him make a living. He's really talented."

"And what makes you say he couldn't have done this?" Laurie asks.

Vince shrugs. "I'm a journalist. Part of my job is knowing people; knowing how they act, how far they can be pushed, what they will do. Just like I know Andy. I know he'll complain and bitch and moan, but at the end of the day, he'll come through for Bobby, and for me."

I turn to Laurie. "Vince thinks I owe him one because he would have done me a favor if I had asked."

She nods. "Sounds about right."

"You're a big help."

Paterson's only full-service hospital isn't actually in Paterson.

St. Joseph's Hospital is located in Wayne, on Hamburg Turnpike. It used to be in Paterson a long time ago, as was Paterson General Hospital and Barnert Hospital. Those two have closed; only St. Joseph's made it out of Paterson alive.

It's fair to say that the demise of the Paterson hospital industry was not due to a lack of sick or injured people. Unfortunately it reflected the overall economic difficulties of the city, a decline from which it has not yet recovered. I've lived here all my life and I love the city, but you rarely see the word *prosperous* connected to it.

I am back at the hospital this morning because this is where my new client still is. The arraignment is taking place here in less than an hour; the justice system determined in its infinite wisdom that it can't wait until Bobby is out of the hospital, especially since doctors say that will be at least two weeks.

A large crowd of media and onlookers are outside the hospital when I get here. This is a huge news story; mayors are not killed every day. I am bombarded with questions as I enter, none of which I answer. Instead I am escorted by a police officer to Bobby's room.

Bobby looks a bit better than the last time I saw him, though that is a low bar to scale. There's more color to his face, and he seems somewhat more alert, but his eyes still have a slightly vacant look.

"Hello, Andy. Is there any news? No one will tell me anything, but I've seen some television. They're all saying I killed the mayor."

"Doesn't matter what they're saying; don't pay attention to it."

"It's just bizarre to know they're talking about me."

"I'm sure it must be."

"Is there anything happening that these reporters don't know about? That they're not saying?" he asks.

"I'm not aware of any new developments, but today is the arraignment. It's going to take place here."

"In this room?"

"No, they set up some kind of conference room on the second floor of the hospital."

"Are you my lawyer?"

"Unless you hired someone else."

"No, but I have to tell you that I have very little money."

"I have very little need for more money." I had already resigned myself to the financial arrangements, or lack of same. I knew that Bobby couldn't afford to pay, and Vince doesn't even pay for his own beer. "Has your memory come back at all?"

"Not about that night, or my accident, no."

"Okay. In terms of the arraignment, they will be asking how you will plead, guilty or not guilty."

"I would never kill anyone."

"Then when they ask you, just say, 'Not guilty, Your Honor.'"

"Okay."

Two nurses and two cops come into the room. The nurses prepare his bed to be moved, and one of them moves the device feeding the IV in his arm alongside the bed. The cops are there to observe, and I assume to make sure that the badly injured Bobby, who is still handcuffed to the bed, doesn't engineer a miraculous escape.

We're brought to the elevator and then down to the second floor. Then the wheeling begins again, until we're brought to what seems to be a conference room, loosely set up as a courtroom.

Everybody is already in place. Judge Stanley Koenig, who is going to preside, is there along with two bailiffs, a court reporter, a court clerk, and a team of four prosecuting attorneys, led by Dylan Campbell. No press or members of the public have been let in, though I'm sure requests must have been made.

No one wants to be here, including me and my client, especially since tomorrow is Thanksgiving and people want to get home. Until now the only place I've ever seen this many unhappy people was at a Knicks game.

Dylan smiles at me when we enter. He and I have gone at it a number of times in courtrooms, not hospital rooms, and I have been lucky enough to win each time. I can tell by the smug smile that he thinks that's about to change.

Judge Koenig quickly takes over, and despite the unconventional surroundings, the arraignment proceeds like any other, which is to say it is uneventful. Bobby performs his role, saying "Not guilty" with as much gusto as he can muster, which isn't much.

I bring up the matter of bail, and it's all Judge Koenig can do not to laugh in my face. It was my obligation to ask for it, but the chance of its being granted ranked slightly lower than the chance Edna will be pleased to hear that we have a client.

I use a few minutes to complain that Dylan has not forwarded any discovery material to the defense: "I assume that the prosecution has what they consider incriminating evidence, or we wouldn't be here. We'd be home basting turkeys."

The judge tells Dylan to get right on it, and he promises he will, while mentioning that tomorrow is a holiday.

I frown at his answer. "Your Honor, if my client can be chained to a bed on this holiday, Mr. Campbell can tell the defense why the government considers that necessary. Besides, if he already has such evidence, he can get it to us today, not tomorrow."

I neglect to mention that I will be eating and watching football tomorrow. Judge Koenig rules that we should start receiving material today, clearly pissing Dylan off. We're off to a good, if typical, start.

The whole thing is over in twenty-five minutes. I again tell Bobby not to talk about the case with anyone, which is probably unnecessary, since he knows nothing about it anyway.

As I'm leaving, Bobby thanks me and then asks me, with fear in his eyes, "Andy, what if I did it?"

I've never been asked that question, and I'm glad that they're wheeling him back to his room so I don't have to answer it.

f I were the Calendar King, I would eliminate every holiday except Thanksgiving, and I'd celebrate it every month.

It is truly the perfect holiday, at least in my house. Family, food, and football . . . which pretty much sums up everything good in the world.

The eating is nothing short of spectacular. It's not just the main meal, which is always outstanding. There are also things to munch on all day, and best of all, Laurie's attitude about my eating habits actually changes for these particular twenty-four hours.

Whereas Laurie was only a lieutenant in the Paterson Police Department, she has since risen to commissioner of the Calorie Police, and in that role she is not hesitant to enforce the law. Yet on Thanksgiving she does not even give me so much as an admonishing stare, no matter what desserts and snacks I suck down.

Then there is the football. Three pro games and two college games spread out throughout the day. It's heaven, and I don't even mind Laurie's Christmas music blaring through the house.

I don't care if "It's Beginning to Look a Lot like Christmas"

intrudes on Tony Romo's analysis, or if I have to listen to Troy
Aikman over the sounds of "Chestnuts Roasting on an Open
Fire." I can totally tune out the gooey music and tune in the
sound of helmets crashing into each other.

And during this entire time I am with Laurie and Ricky,
my two absolutely favorite people, as well as my three favorite dogs. During halftime of some of the games Ricky
and I go outside and throw a football in the driveway. He's
only twelve and already throws a tighter spiral than I ever
did. In a few years Nick Saban is going to be standing in
this driveway with us, recruiting him.

"Sorry, Nick," I'll say with a smug smile on my face.
"He's going to Michigan."

Of course, this Thanksgiving is less perfect than most.
That is because hovering over everything is the existence
of the dreaded "client." When it is over, when Al Michaels
signs off at the end of the Steelers-Ravens game tonight, I
will have to go back to the real world.

I hope the game goes into overtime.

Sitting in the den are two boxes of discovery documents,
which arrived last night. Dylan obviously took Judge Koenig's directive seriously and got his office moving on it. I
wish I hadn't been so insistent, since now I feel an obligation to look through all of them.

When the game ends, I take Tara, Sebastian, and Hunter
for a quick walk and then I open the first box. My plan is
to only spend a few minutes getting the lay of the land,
but that turns into an hour and a half.

It doesn't take nearly that long to see why the police
arrested Bobby Nash so quickly. Mayor Oliva's wife reported that she received two calls from Bobby, one the day

of the murder and one the day before, both demanding a meeting with her husband.

She described the calls as borderline threatening if the mayor didn't agree, and she recommended to her husband that he call the police. Since as the mayor the police reported to him, they would then take the appropriation action without having to be told twice.

According to her, Oliva considered bringing in the police, but was reluctant to deal with the publicity it might generate if the news got out. The police records do not show that he ever made the report.

A neighbor reported seeing a running car parked near the mayor's house at an odd angle. The neighbor had never seen it there before, and no parking is allowed on that street after 8:00 P.M. It was strange enough to him that he took down the license plate number. It was Bobby Nash's car.

The blood in the trunk of the car was the final straw, and although the tests had not been done when the arrest was made, the results showed that it was in fact the mayor's blood.

There seems to be a lot more in here about Bobby's often-expressed dislike for the mayor, and the incident with the false newspaper article. The mayor's and Minchner's threatened lawsuits are mentioned, as is Bobby's subsequent firing. The prosecution will not have to prove motive, but the jury will undoubtedly hear all of this, and that will look bad for Bobby.

Reading these documents is such a miserable experience that I momentarily don't notice the strains of "Rudolph the Red-Nosed Reindeer" playing in the house.

All in all, this is not the way I had hoped to end the perfect holiday.

Vince's voice on the phone again sounds desperate.

"Andy, I spoke to Bobby. You've got to do me a favor."

"Do you a favor? What do you think I've been doing? I'm taking on a case which could cause me to work my ass off for months, and which might cost me tens of thousands of dollars. And now you're asking me for a favor?"

"That is one favor; this is an entirely different one. You need to learn to compartmentalize."

"Vince, let me tell you what you need to do. You need to—"

He interrupts, probably because he knew what was coming. "Seriously, I really need help, and it's right up your alley. Otherwise I wouldn't ask."

I sigh loudly, for effect, though I know it will have no impact on Vince. "What is it now?"

"Bobby asked me to take his dog while he's in jail. His neighbor had it, but they can't keep it 'cause they're renting and the landlord said no."

"What did you tell him?"

"What could I say? He's under arrest and in the hospital; how could I not be there for him? Of course I said yes. Don't you have some kind of dog place where I could keep the thing?"

Vince is referring to the Tara Foundation, a rescue organization that a partner and I run. "No, Vince. That's for dogs looking for homes. Bobby's *thing* has a home . . . yours. Until Bobby can take it back, if he can take it back. Is it a male for female?"

"What's the difference?"

"What's the difference between a male and a female? I assume you haven't had a date in a while?"

"I mean why does it matter to you?"

"It doesn't; I just don't like calling a dog 'it.'"

"You're a strange one, Andy. But I don't know what it is. Should I look?"

"You have the dog with you now?"

"Yeah. The name is Duchess, so it's probably a girl."

"What kind of dog is it?"

"Bobby said it was a golden retriever, or a mix, or something."

"How big and how old?"

"What are you, writing a book about this dog?" Vince snarls. "Will you take it or not?"

"No. How big and how old?"

"I think he said four months, and it's really big."

"She's going to get a lot bigger."

"Bigger than this? Is there anything I can do? Can I stop her from growing?"

"Sure. Start her smoking cigarettes."

"Andy, just take the damn dog. . . . I'm begging you."

"Which part of *no* don't you understand? But I'll tell

you what. I'll ask Sondra to help you get started, show you the right food, tell you how to set up your house, everything you need to know."

"Who's Sondra?"

"Willie Miller's wife; she helps run the foundation."

"Come on, Andy. What am I going to do with a dog?"

"Love her and be loved. Well, I doubt she'll love you; but hopefully you'll get to a point where she'll tolerate you."

"When will Sondra be here?"

"I'll call her now."

Vince doesn't say anything for a few moments, then, "What is it? . . . *Oh my God . . . it shit on the floor!*"

I can't help it; I laugh out loud. Then, "You need to walk her, Vince."

"It shit on the floor! In my house! The floor I walk on!"

"Vince, I've been in your house. It's a pigsty; I'm surprised you even noticed what she did."

"I have lived here for ten years! And you know what hasn't happened in ten years? Nobody has ever shit on the floor!"

"I'm calling Sondra, Vince. Just clean it up and then wait for Sondra to call you."

I hang up and already feel guilty that I'm about to do this to poor Sondra. But what I am really upset about is that I'm not there to watch Vince pick it up.

This is an unusual way for me to enter a case.

I've given up trying to fully retire; as much as I don't go after clients, they seem to show up at my door and force their way in. I'm getting used to that, and I've come to accept my fate.

But what generally happens is that the situation presents itself and I come to a conscious, albeit often sudden, decision to take on the case. I've thought it through, considered the variables, and jumped in. Almost always reluctantly—usually while being coerced—but always intentionally.

This time has been different. I sort of oozed my way into representing Bobby Nash. It started as a favor to Vince and just gradually seemed to happen. I could have said no at any point along the way, but instead I took some refuge in simply the absence of yes. But that wasn't enough, and here I am.

The case, even to my defense attorney's eyes, is a disaster waiting to happen. Or more accurately a disaster that has already happened.

The evidence is daunting, but I'm used to that. Just as worrisome is a client who has no idea what happened, and who is willing to entertain the possibility that he might have done it. The best he can do is say that a murder is something he doubts he could commit; it's possible that juries will not find that particularly compelling.

When I gather our legal team together to start a case, I generally try to summon enough fake enthusiasm to get them eager to tackle the job ahead. I don't often have much to tell them because it's by definition early in the process. I just want them prepared for what is to come.

So that's what I'm going to do right now, as I look around the room at the assembled group. I doubt they're going to be surprised to hear that our client is the guy accused of the mayor's murder; they know Bobby's connection to Vince, and Vince's connection to me.

We're sitting at the conference table in my office on Van Houten Street. There is nothing at all impressive about the setting. The office is on the second floor above a fruit stand, and the conference room, such as it is, is barely large enough to hold the entire table. There can't be a chair at one of the ends or we would not be able to close the door.

I'm standing, and to my immediate left is Edna. She usually tries to position herself near the door so she can be the first one out, but she arrived later than usual today. She was probably busy planning her wedding, or buying cruise wear.

Next to her is Sam Willis. In real life he is my accountant and has an office down the hall, but in legal life he's our computer guy. His talent is being able to hack, legally and especially illegally, into pretty much any computer system ever invented.

Next to Sam is Laurie and then Marcus Clark, one of three members, along with Corey Douglas and Laurie, of the K Team. They are our investigators and are outstanding at what they do. Marcus is the most frightening human being in this or any other galaxy, and he is tougher than he is scary. He says little, and what he does say is impossible for anyone other than Laurie to understand, yet he never has trouble getting his point across.

Marcus is on our side and has saved me on many occasions, yet I am still nervous every time I am with him.

Next to Marcus is Corey Douglas. Corey is a retired Paterson cop, and he and his German shepherd K-9 partner, Simon Garfunkel, round out the K Team. Simon is also here, but he is asleep in my office. Simon finds these meetings even more boring than I do.

To Corey's left is Willie Miller. Willie is a former client of mine and my current partner in a dog rescue operation called the Tara Foundation. He and his wife, Sondra, basically run the place. Since I sent Sondra to deal with Vince, I am surprised that Willie is still talking to me.

Willie is not technically part of our team, but other than Marcus he is the toughest, most fearless person I know, so he helps out a lot on special assignments.

Last is Eddie Dowd, the only other lawyer in the group. Eddie is a relative newcomer to us, but I knew of him in his days playing football for the New York Giants. He's a terrific lawyer and a good guy, even if he talks almost exclusively in sports clichés.

"Our client is Bobby Nash," I say. "Unless you have been residing in a cave without TV or internet all week, you know he is accused of killing Mayor Alex Oliva."

"Is he going to take a plea bargain?" Edna asks, ever hopeful.

"That is not under consideration at this point. He's in

the hospital with injuries suffered in a car crash. Complicating matters is that he remembers nothing about the time in question."

"Head injury?" Corey asks.

"He did suffer a concussion. But the police say there are drugs involved, and the toxicology report confirms it. Bobby denies ever using drugs, and Vince swears he is telling the truth about it. Obviously, Vince could be wrong."

"So what's our game plan?" Eddie asks.

"I have no idea at this point; I just don't know enough. For now I guess we try to find out what happened to Bobby that night; maybe what he is forgetting is that he was dining with the queen of England. Sam, start on that, check Bobby's credit card records and the GPS on his phone. It would be great if we could show he was elsewhere.

"Also, according to the mayor's wife, Bobby called the mayor twice to make threats, once the day he was killed and once the day before. She answered both calls; the mayor was not at home. Please check Bobby's phone records to see if he actually made those calls."

I turn back to the group. "We'll also have to find out who else would have wanted to kill the mayor."

"That makes me a suspect," Corey says.

"You're not a fan?"

"There's not a cop in New Jersey who is a fan."

"So let's find somebody who dislikes him enough to put a bullet in him."

Mayor Alex Oliva was widely liked by the people who didn't know him.

He won with 70 percent of the vote when he ran for a second term and had since made no secret of his intention to run for governor in next November's election. With the current governor term limited, Oliva was considered one of the favorites, and early polls gave him a small lead.

His main competition in that election was expected to be Aaron Widener, a state senator from Elizabeth. I would imagine that Widener will now take the lead in that race.

In public Oliva had that "it" factor that politicians are either born with or never acquire. He could be tough, charming, demanding, self-deprecating, and compassionate. Little of it was real, but it came across exactly as intended.

But among those who worked closely with him, and especially those who served under him, he was both disliked and feared. I ironically know this through Vince, whose newspaper covered him, and who couldn't stand him. I had almost no personal contact with Oliva, other than at a few charity dinners. I try to limit my exposure to politicians to a bare minimum; they trigger my hypocrite allergy.

On the positive side, Oliva ran for mayor promising to clean up Paterson politics, no easy task. Paterson has rarely been pointed to as a model of clean government and untainted politics. Not long ago a mayor was jailed for corruption, and a recent election for the City Council was ruled fraudulent and invalidated by the courts.

Paterson received unwanted national attention when Donald Trump, during his reelection campaign, used the city as an example of what can and does go wrong in elections. He said that voters should look at Paterson, "where massive percentages of the vote was a fraud."

Oliva was having some apparent success rooting out those in city government who in his view had less than stellar reputations and was at least making things more transparent. The jury was still out on whether the changes were actual improvements, but he trumpeted them as major triumphs.

But while Vince has been telling me about Oliva for a while now, he has always expressed frustration that he couldn't get anyone to go on the record about what Oliva was really like. I also suspect that Vince's disdain for him was a contributing cause for Vince's approving Bobby Nash's story without checking it as carefully as necessary; certainly Vince's dislike for Oliva was heightened by the results of that incident.

Pete Stanton has also talked to me about Oliva, so Corey's negative view did not surprise me. According to Pete, Oliva was not a friend to the department and the cops in it, laying blame whenever he could, and trying to avoid paying them a fair salary.

But the kind of people that felt that way about Oliva— city commissioners, public employees, and the like—are generally not the types to put a bullet in his back and leave him in a park. Of course, according to Vince, Bobby is not that type either.

The park is where our involvement in the case will begin. Laurie and I always go to the scene of the crime, just to get a feel for it. I don't bring her because it's a husband-and-wife romantic thing; we don't generally call each other pet names as we look at the bloodstains. I bring her because she's an outstanding investigator and has a better eye for this stuff than I do.

I've been to this particular scene before, when Tara discovered the body. But it was night, and snow covered, and we were prevented by the police from looking closely at the area once they arrived. Today we'll try to make up for that.

Technically this is not the murder scene; it is simply where the body was found. It seems unlikely that he was shot here; the discovery claims that he was shot in his own driveway. Since it's a long shot that his wife would welcome us to their home, we're coming here instead.

Fortunately, the weather has turned warmer and the snow has mostly melted. Unfortunately, the scene has turned into what can only be described as a social meeting place.

As we walk into the park, the place where we found the body is about fifty feet from the tennis courts. The nets have been removed and the courts are empty because of the winter weather, but the fencing around the courts has been turned into a shrine for the recently departed mayor. Patersonians have left flowers, poems, and mementos in his honor; it's a chain-link wailing wall.

Also at least fifty people must be milling around; they seem to have found a sense of community in their grief, and some are actually sobbing. Others hold up candles or have placed them on the wooden stands near the courts.

Cops surround the place where the body actually was, blocking people from getting too close. I'm not sure why, since the forensics people have long ago done their work, and the melting snow has obliterated everything anyway. Maybe they're just treating it as sacred ground.

Once again, it's Laurie to the rescue. She goes over to talk to one of the cops that she knows, and we're ushered onto the hallowed patch of grass. I'm aware that we're standing on the very spot where Sebastian took a piss, so I'm not overcome with reverence and emotion.

If not for the cops and the crowds and the tributes, there would not be the slightest indication that anything happened here. No chalk outline of a body, no traces of blood, no fingerprint powder, nothing at all. It does not look like a murder scene; it looks like a piece of Eastside Park.

"You were walking on the road?" Laurie asks.

I nod. "Yes. It had been plowed, so that's where we were. Right over there is where David was telling me about Edna's incredible work ethic, while I tried not to gag."

"And Tara detected something and ran from there?"

"Right . . . at first I thought it must be a squirrel. I followed her, and David followed me with Sebastian and Hunter."

"Were there footprints along the way? Or maybe signs of something being dragged?"

"Something like a body?"

"Something like that."

I have to think about it for a while and try to reconstruct what I saw that night. I was a little concerned about Tara running off, but I remember running through the fairly deep snow after her. "There was nothing," I say. "The snow had not been touched; at least, not that I remember."

"Then the body must have been left here before the snow started. The killer probably drove off the road in the dark and came here, rather than drag the body all the way. The ground would have been mostly frozen, so the car could have navigated it easily."

"So we need to find out when it actually started snowing; maybe Bobby was still in the bar at that point."

She nods. "Right."

"The other thing is that it snowed much more than they predicted; right up until the time it started they were saying maybe three inches."

"So?"

"So the killer was not hiding the body; he was perfectly content with it being discovered right away. He could have taken it twenty feet farther into the woods, and it might not have been found for a day or two."

I'm not sure if that realization helps us or hurts us; we won't know until we learn more. Right now it's just a fact to file away.

"We're only a few blocks from Oliva's house," I say. He lives on Thirty-ninth and Park, right down the block from where we're standing.

"Was he abducted and shot at his house?"

"Apparently so, at least according to the discovery. There are still some forensics that we haven't received yet."

"If he was, then the killer didn't waste any time. He just killed him and dumped him here. Impulsive."

I don't bother saying so, but we both know that could be consistent with someone strung out on drugs, which the cops allege about Bobby.

Unfortunately, Laurie does bother saying so. "So their theory is Bobby took drugs, maybe mixed with alcohol from his time at the bar, abducted the mayor, killed and dumped him here after putting his body in the trunk. Then he realized he was in trouble, took off, and crashed his car."

"But why move him in the first place? Why wouldn't the killer just leave him where he was shot, rather than take the trouble to put him into the trunk and drive a few blocks to dump him?"

"Good question."

I nod. "Dylan will have to be able to explain it to the jury. It's a complication to an otherwise nice, clean theory."

"Jury? Is this going to go to trial?"

"Not if Edna can help it."

Theresa Minardo had thought it was over.

It had been four months since the story broke about the mayor, and three months since Bobby Nash's firing led to the withdrawal of the lawsuit. She certainly had some regrets about her role in it, but the damage was contained, and she would argue that the greater good had been enhanced.

The murder of the mayor, and Nash's subsequent arrest, changed everything. Not only did it rob the state and the country of a potential political star, but it brought her back into the media spotlight.

That spotlight is shining far brighter than it had before. Oliva's death is not a local story; it is national news. Even though the police have placed the guilt at the feet of a vengeful reporter, national outlets are seeing it as a symptom of political violence, brought about by hyper-partisanship.

Theresa had been avoiding the calls and requests for interviews and had not left her house. One reason for that was her having a pretty bad case of the flu, so she would not have gone out anyway. She could barely keep anything down and had been existing on soup and tea.

The press had been camped outside her house since the

mayor's death, waiting for her to appear so they could photograph her and lob questions in her direction. She had no intention of answering the reporters, but their mere presence stressed her out.

A few times she considered going outside and announcing that she was not going to answer their questions, so they might as well leave. She didn't know if that would work and doubted that it would. The whole idea of going out there scared her, so she kept putting it off.

Theresa had followed the coverage on television. It was weird and disconcerting to sit in her house and see it on the television screen. This was not a story that she wanted to be a part of.

Theresa had no idea at all whether Bobby Nash was guilty. She hoped that he was; that he was of a type to commit murder certainly made her feel less bad that she had damaged his career, even though she had to recognize that the damage she did may well have driven him over the edge. If it did, she rationalized, then he must have been close to that edge all along.

But the main reason she was rooting for Bobby's guilt was that she knew other people were intent on derailing the mayor's career. She did not know why that was, but she certainly suspected that they were dangerous, and that they would go to great lengths to get what they wanted.

Theresa was finished with them, and glad of it.

Hovering over this entire situation was the simple fact that life goes on and she now needed a job. A committee to elect someone does not have a need for many employees when the person they are trying to get elected is dead.

The bottom line was that as much as Theresa dreaded it,

it was time to reenter the world. She wanted to go down to the committee office and find out what everyone was saying, and what people's job prospects were. They would know who was hiring political operatives for the upcoming election season. Theresa knew that campaigns were things to be jumped on early.

On a more basic level, she needed to go to the market and stock up on food.

She developed a plan for avoiding the reporters. The leaving would be fairly easy. Her car was in the attached garage, so they would not see her leave the house or enter the garage. Once inside, she'd turn on the car, quickly use the garage door opener, and exit quickly.

She'd go at a good speed down her driveway. The reporters wouldn't dare get in front of the car, and she'd be gone before they could react. At least that was the plan.

Getting back would be more difficult, though it would still involve a game of chicken, not stopping and hoping the reporters would stay out of the way as she drove into the garage.

So Theresa grabbed her purse and went through the laundry room door into the closed garage. She knew the media people in front of her house couldn't hear her, but she still tried to be as quiet as possible.

She got into her car, took a deep breath, and grabbed the garage door opener with her left hand. She held her key in the other hand and turned on the car. It seemed like a loud roar to her, but still wouldn't be loud enough to alert the people out front.

Either way it wouldn't matter; she was coming out fast and it was going to be up to them to steer clear of her.

Another deep breath and she pressed the garage door opener. The explosion sent the top of the garage shooting skyward.

It would prove impossible for the coroner and forensics people to definitely determine, but it was extremely unlikely that she was alive when the fireball consumed her body.

The media assembled in front of Theresa's house had stumbled on more of a story than they expected. But one thing they would not be doing was interviewing Theresa Minardo.

Today is perhaps the single most dreaded day of the year—tree decoration day.

Thanks to my case, I got out of the second most dreaded day—tree purchasing day—yesterday. Laurie had taken Ricky, and they picked one out; I think Laurie has grown tired of me complaining about their looking at every tree in the place before settling on one. My position always struck me as reasonable, since every tree looked exactly the same.

But the decorating is the absolute worst. Laurie insists that every single square inch of the tree be covered with either a light or an ornament. And Ricky, traitor that he is, goes along with it, even though this invariably takes place during a football game.

They don't recognize that completely inundating the tree with lights and trinkets, thereby obscuring every bit of said tree, makes their endless debate over which tree to get even more ridiculous.

But my son chooses to put plastic reindeer on a tree rather than watch Wake Forest play North Carolina. It is a fact of life that I have to learn to deal with, but that doesn't make it any less painful. Where have I gone wrong? Can I fairly place all the blame on Laurie?

The tree decorating takes forever. My view, which is not

shared by anyone else in this house, is that a single halftime should provide plenty of opportunity for filling up the tree with junk. Once the third quarter begins, that should be it. Whatever shape the tree is in should be good enough.

Mercifully, in recent years my participation has not been required. In fact, I am pretty much unwelcome. They got tired of my whining and looking at my watch and also disapproved of my ornament placement. It seemed like wherever I put one was wrong.

I'm fine with being excluded, believe me, but they have gotten a bit mean about it. I believe the phrase Laurie used last year was "Get the hell out of this room and don't come back." Does she not realize that 'tis the season to be jolly? Fa-la-la-la-la?

The halftime of the Georgia-Tennessee game is interrupted for "breaking news." I have long since stopped believing that "breaking news" was significant, or even "breaking." News stations have taken to assigning that characterization to everything, no matter how dated or trivial.

But this one is worthy of the chyron: a woman's garage has blown up, killing her. It takes a couple of minutes, but they come up with a tentative identification.

Theresa Minardo.

"Laurie, come in here." I guess the tone of my voice is weird enough that she actually stops decorating and joins me.

She sees that I'm watching the news. After about thirty seconds she says, "Theresa Minardo? Isn't that the woman—"

"One and the same."

"How awful."

Of course it is awful, whether or not she set Bobby up

for that story. I usually feel we should mourn the dead for at least ten minutes before trying to come up with ways to take advantage of it, but I'm going to make an exception in this case. "But it could help us."

"Because if Bobby is in jail, then someone else is out there murdering people."

"Right. Unless the device was planted a while ago, before Bobby was arrested."

"That would be unfortunate."

"One way to find out." I pick up the phone and dial Pete Stanton's cell phone.

He answers, instead of saying hello, "I win the pool."

"What does that mean?"

"The over/under on how long it would take for you to call me once the Minardo killing hit the media was fifteen minutes. I had the under, so I win. Easy money."

"Congratulations. I win also because my client is in jail and couldn't have done it."

"Sorry, counselor. The victim hasn't used her car in more than a week. So the over/under on how long it will take Dylan to try and charge your boy with a second homicide is twenty minutes. I'm taking the under again."

I hang up and share the bad news with Laurie. Ten minutes later the phone rings, and Eddie Dowd tells me that we've just been notified of an additional search warrant being served on Bobby Nash's house.

Dylan is definitely already trying to tie Bobby to the Theresa Minardo murder.

Pete wins his under bet again.

I t's back to the hospital today for arraignment number two.

This breaks my personal case record for most arraignments in a hospital; my previous high was zero.

Last night we got some amended discovery information and included in it were the results of the second search warrant served at Bobby's house. Eddie Dowd was there to observe, and he said that although they weren't telling him anything, they seemed very interested in the basement.

The discovery explains exactly what that interest was about. Trace explosives were found in the work area. It was the same type of explosive that blew up Theresa Minardo's garage, with Theresa Minardo in it. That was more than enough to add her murder to the list of charges against Bobby Nash.

So once again I am starting the prearraignment conversation with Bobby. He's a captive audience, since he's still cuffed to the hospital bed.

"How are you feeling?" is my opening salvo.

"I saw the news about Theresa Minardo on television. Is that why you're here?"

He didn't answer my question. If he tried that on the witness stand, I would complain to the judge, but in this case I appreciate his directness. No sense tiptoeing around this.

"Yes. You're being charged with her murder as well."

"How could that be? I've been in here . . . chained to the bed. How could I possibly have killed her?"

"They think the device was planted before you were arrested."

He moans his displeasure at that. "Well, I did not do this. I could not have lost that much memory. Why do they think it's me? Because she set me up on the story?"

I nod. "That, and because they found trace explosives in your basement."

Suddenly he is by far the most animated I have seen him. "No. There is no chance of that. I did not have explosives. I did not make a bomb. How the hell would I know how to make a bomb? I can't even make myself breakfast."

"So your plea will be not guilty?"

"Damn right," he says, for the first time showing anger along with the fear. "It's one thing if I blacked out and did something that I don't remember. I don't think that happened, but I admit it's possible. This is not possible; I would have had to buy explosive material, build a bomb, and then plant the damn bomb. I did not do that while I was blacked out; I wouldn't know how to do that conscious or unconscious. I did not do that at all."

I'm actually experiencing a feeling of relief. I don't want a client, but if I'm stuck with one, it's important that I believe in his or her innocence. I'm spoiled, because having enough money not to work means I don't have to fight for a guilty person's freedom. I was afraid that was what I was doing here; now I'm changing my mind.

"Good," I say. "Let's kick their ass."

We start the procession down the hallway again, Bobby, me, the nurses shepherding the IV tubes along, and the cops guarding the whole thing. This time the word must have gotten around because patients, nurses, doctors, and even visitors are lined up along the parade route.

The scene in the conference courtroom is the same as last time, except now there are a few members of the press. The collective press had complained about being shut out last time, so they probably let in a delegation on behalf of the entire press pool. They will no doubt share what they have seen and heard.

Eddie Dowd is already at the defense table. I had him come this time because now I am sure this is going to trial, where last time I wasn't.

Dylan sees me come in, but instead of just smiling his obnoxious smile, he comes over to me. "Here we go again."

I don't answer; so far this doesn't seem like a conversation worth pursuing.

"We have anything to talk about?"

"You mean like recipes or good books we read on vacation?" He's asking if I want to discuss a plea deal, and I'm telling him that I don't.

He smiles, undaunted. "Okay, you know where I am if you want to reach me, but you wouldn't like what I have to say anyway. I mean, we're talking about the mayor."

"Dylan, I'm going to do you a favor because I like . . . doing favors. Tell the judge that you made a mistake and that you're dropping the charges. It will save you an embarrassing loss . . . another embarrassing loss."

He laughs, but I'm pretty sure he didn't think what I said was funny. "I'll take my chances."

Judge Koenig convenes the hearing, which moves even faster than last time. Bobby once again pleads not guilty, this time in a stronger and more decisive voice.

I don't bother asking for bail, since it's already been denied once. Adding another murder charge doesn't exactly make Bobby's bail argument stronger, and prolonging the hearing would likely only piss Judge Koenig off.

I will have plenty of opportunity to piss him off during the trial.

When it's over, I turn to Bobby. "Don't be in a hurry to get out of here. It's more comfortable than a jail cell, and the nurses are much friendlier."

"Okay."

"Let me know if you hear they are going to move you, and I'll tell the court that you're not physically able to handle it. Might buy you a week or two."

"Great . . . thanks. And, Andy, I really didn't do this."

"I believe you, but this is not an accident; somebody has been setting you up. Spend some time thinking about who and why."

'm comforted by the fact that these two murders make no sense to me. At least not as a pair.

They couldn't be more different. The killing of Mayor Oliva was cold and brutal, an execution committed at close range. It feels impulsive; he was grabbed and quickly killed and dumped in a nearby park.

Theresa Minardo's murder is the opposite. That was carefully planned, done from a distance on probably a specific timetable; it would take place after the mayor's death, but at a time and in a way that Bobby could still have committed it. When she opened the garage door, she was going to die; once the device was placed, the timing was up to her and apparently of little consequence to her killer.

All that the killings had in common was that Bobby had an apparent motive in both cases, and no alibi. He either committed the murders or he was set up to take the fall; his presence in this case is no accident.

I told Bobby to think about who could be setting him up, but it likely isn't about Bobby at all. Bobby is a convenient and credible person to blame; he is simply the vehicle by which the real killer can stay in the clear.

I know little about the lives of the victims; I am starting from square one. But my instinct is that this is about the mayor, and that the Minardo killing was a tragic icing on the cake meant to cement the appearance of Bobby's guilt.

I may turn out to be wrong about that, but that's my best guess at the moment. The mayor played in a high-stakes world; he controlled money and power, and that would be multiplied tenfold if he won the governorship, as appeared likely. Those kinds of things create motives for murder.

Maybe Theresa Minardo will have connections to a dangerous world, but it seems more likely that this is about the mayor. It also seems unlikely that we will be able to prove, or even create reasonable doubt, that Bobby didn't commit these crimes without coming up with a credible alternative for who did.

While I'm driving home from the hospital, Sam calls me on my cell. "Hey, Andy. I've run the check on Bobby's credit cards and phone GPS."

"What did you come up with?"

"You're not going to like most of it."

For some reason Sam always feels it necessary to predict how I am going to react to whatever news he has for me. I always find it annoying, but much more so when his prediction is negative.

"Just tell me, Sam."

"The credit cards do nothing for us. He paid his bill at the Crow's Nest that night, but that was the only time he used them in the forty-eight hours before and after the mayor's murder."

"What else?"

"Here comes the bad part. He, or at least his phone, was at the mayor's house that night, and also in Eastside Park around the estimated time of death."

"Damn." Sam can access the phone company computers that show where cell phones are at all times, since they have GPS devices within them. We could get the information legally, but this saves time. If it shows what we want, then we subpoena the same records. If not, we don't get the records through the proper channels. This unfortunately does not show what we want.

"He still had it with him when he crashed the car, and in fact it's still with him at the hospital."

"You're full of good news."

"Actually, I have a couple of positive things for you. I went back three weeks on the GPS. He was not at Theresa Minardo's house, or at least his phone wasn't. And I checked on the mayor's wife's claim that Bobby called him twice."

"And?"

"If he did, he didn't use his own phone."

I thank Sam and end the call. That last part about Bobby not being at the Minardo house is helpful, although Dylan will argue that Bobby probably just didn't have his phone with him when he planted the explosive.

The rest of Sam's overall message is close to a disaster. Bobby's phone being at the mayor's house and the park is devastating. We cannot claim that it was stolen because it is still in his possession.

If Dylan gets the GPS phone records, and I have no doubt that he will, we have a big problem.

I have an idea, so I call Sam back. "Sam, you said that Bobby's phone was never at Theresa Minardo's house."

"Right."

"Can you tell which phones were there? Can you cross-check it by location rather than phone, meaning if a cell phone was there, you could find a record of it?"

"Sure," he says without hesitation. "But—"

"I hate the word *but,* Sam."

"I know, but—"

"You just used it again."

"Sorry. I was just going to point out that this is not all that exact. I can tell you what phones were at her house, for sure, but I also might pick up phones that were at the houses next door, for example."

"What about in cars that were just driving by?"

"No, they wouldn't have been there long enough. If they show up, I can weed them out. How far back should I go?"

I don't know exactly how long it was that Theresa did not use her car, so I don't want to cut it too close. "Let's say two weeks. Can you do that?"

"I can, but it will take a while. I'll do it as fast as I can."

"Thanks, Sam."

The Oliva for Governor organization has had a tough week.

It was left without a reason for existing when Oliva was killed, then another of their own, Theresa Minardo, suffered the same fate. None of the others, not the idealists and not the pragmatic political operatives, signed up for anything like this.

I have to assume that the rank and file in the organization admired Oliva. They worked for his success in jobs that cannot pay much money. I'm sure some of them were hoping to ride his ascent to their own positions of power within the state government, but that doesn't negate that they chose the candidate that they wanted to win and thought had a good chance.

Theresa Minardo was one of those people. She was with Oliva from day one, meaning going back to when he was first running for mayor of Paterson. She had a significant position within the campaign organization; she would certainly have been considered part of top management.

The main office for the campaign is on Market Street in Paterson. The large storefront used to house a furniture store. As I pull up, I see the campaign posters are still in the window; maybe nobody has the heart or inclination to take them down.

I'm here to see Katie Corneau, who was a publicity spokesperson in the organization for Oliva. In that position she knew Vince, who has set up this meeting. He said that she was reluctant to talk to me, but was doing so as a favor to Vince. I can speak from personal experience when I say that Vince is a hard man to say no to.

When I talked to Vince to arrange this, he started and ended the call by pleading with me to take "the dog." "She's driving me crazy, Andy. She chewed up a roll of toilet paper."

"She's a puppy, Vince."

"So all puppies chew toilet paper? That's a puppy thing?"

"Yes, that's a definite puppy thing."

"Maybe she should save the toilet paper to use when she shits on the floor."

"She's still doing that?"

"No, because I walk her all the time. I've gone through three pairs of shoes walking her."

I finally manage to get off the phone. Sondra had been over there the other day trying to help him, and yesterday she told me that she was worried for Vince's sanity. That ship, I assured her, had already sailed.

I open the door to the campaign office and go inside. A half dozen people are there, mostly working at their desks. They're probably just putting the finishing touches on things, but if I didn't know that Oliva was dead, I would think it was business as usual.

A young woman looks up at me from her desk and nods in my direction. She stands up and silently points to a door in the back, signaling that I should join her back there, which I do.

She explains, even though it isn't necessary, "I'm Katie Corneau. I'm sorry for the secrecy, but Bobby Nash is not a very popular person around here, and since you're his lawyer . . ."

"I understand. Thank you for talking with me."

"Vince is pretty persuasive. He asked me for two favors: one was to talk to you, and the other was to take care of some dog. This seemed like the easier one."

"You spent a lot of time with the mayor?"

"I wouldn't say a lot, though much more lately. The campaign was going to be getting into high gear, so he was becoming more hands-on. And I handled publicity, which is second only to fundraising as the name of the game."

"Theresa Minardo was on the fundraising side?"

Katie nods. "Yes, but more than that. She was actually in charge of publicity as well; she was my boss as well as my friend."

"I'm more interested in her fundraising role."

"She was amazing at it. She'd set a donor up, then have the mayor speak to them to close the deal." Katie smiles. "Theresa had no shame; she'd ask anyone for anything. That's the way you have to be in those jobs."

"You were here back when Bobby Nash ran that story about the donor?"

"Of course."

"What did you think when the story first ran? I mean, before it was shown to be false."

Katie hesitates. "I guess I believed it. Well, I shouldn't say that. Let's just say I believed it could be true. Money is oxygen in politics; a million dollars lets you breathe for a while."

"It would have been an illegal contribution, a quid pro quo for the construction contract."

She nods. "You think that would have made it unique? Anyway, bottom line is, it wasn't true. Your client made the whole thing up."

"So you believed Theresa Minardo when she said she had nothing to do with it?"

"Of course. Why would she try and hurt Alex's political career? That would have been self-destructive on a number of levels."

I note her casual use of the mayor's first name; they were obviously close. "He used the incident to attack the media; I assume you helped orchestrate that?"

She smiles. "Of course; who likes the media? But in this case they deserved what they got, once it was proven that the story wasn't supported. It wound up working big-time in our favor; Alex came out smelling like a rose."

"Was the feeling around here that Bobby Nash deliberately lied? Or was he manipulated?"

"I think most people here who are not involved in the publicity end of things think he lied. I think he lied about Theresa, but I also thought he was manipulated by people trying to sandbag Alex. Now I'm not so sure what to think; someone who could commit murder is capable of anything."

"Let me ask you this. If you found out tomorrow, beyond any doubt, that Bobby Nash didn't do this, who would be on your list of suspects?"

I expect a knee-jerk reaction insisting that Bobby is guilty, but instead she thinks about it for a few moments. "If it was just Alex, it would be a long list. He had a lot of political enemies because he challenged business as usual; he was cleaning up this town and would have done the same for the state. I'm not saying all of those enemies are murderers, but he was a threat to them.

"But killing Theresa . . . that changes the equation. She had no enemies, and she had no intention of hurting anyone. The fact that they both were victims . . . I'm afraid that points to your client."

I think she's right, and I think that might be exactly why Theresa Minardo was killed.

That's not possible; I was never at Alex Oliva's house. I don't even know where he lived. And why would I have gone to the park?"

I can hear the frustration in Bobby's voice; I've just told him Sam's news that Bobby's phone was at Oliva's house and then Eastside Park the night of the murder. His world is closing in on him and he doesn't know why. Or the world is closing in on him and he does know why . . . because he's guilty.

Either way, he knows he's in major trouble.

Physically, Bobby is improving. He's off the IVs and getting around pretty well. I'm afraid that fairly soon they're going to move him to the jail; I'll ask Eddie Dowd to file a motion with the court to delay it when the time comes, but that will only be a temporary reprieve at best.

"Well, your phone knows where he lived," I say. "And we know from the witness that your car knows it also; a neighbor saw it parked there."

"You don't believe me?"

"Actually, I do. Not sure why, but I don't have time to analyze it. The important thing is that the phone and the car . . . these are facts, and we have to accept them and explain them."

"To the jury?"

"First to ourselves. We need to know what is going on before we can expect the jury to accept our position."

"I have no idea what is going on," he says.

"Join the club. Tell me about your relationship with Theresa Minardo."

"There was no relationship. I had never met her until she came to me."

"She called you?"

"No. I was covering an Oliva press conference. She came up to me and told me that we needed to meet, that she had information I would be very interested in."

"Why did she pick you?"

Bobby frowns. "I've thought about that a lot. I think it was because I was inexperienced and could be fooled. She was right about that."

"So you met her? Where?"

"Yes; ironically, we met in Eastside Park. She told me that she had believed in Oliva for a long time, but that she had learned some things about him, and that her conscience couldn't handle it. She told me about Minchner and the million dollars; she said that Minchner was a crook and that he would own Oliva when he became governor."

"What did you tell her?"

"That I needed proof and I would need her to come forward. She said that she would get me the proof, but that coming forward would ruin her future career. No politician would ever trust her or want her in their organization again."

"What happened next?"

"I received an envelope in the mail . . . no return address, but it was obviously from Theresa. It contained the copies of the checks. I confirmed that they came from a company that Minchner controlled, and that they were drawn on that company's bank. So I went with the story. You know the rest; it blew up in my face."

"And she denied everything." It's a statement, not a question.

He nods. "Right. She had said she wouldn't admit it publicly, and she didn't."

"Any idea why she wanted the story out in the first place?"

"Obviously she was trying to sandbag Oliva; this couldn't have been about me. I wasn't . . . I'm not . . . important enough. But I can't be sure if she knew the checks were fake. My guess is that she did, since her job was fundraising. But I suppose someone could have been using her by slipping her bad information. I just don't know; she refused to talk to me when it all went south."

"She continued to work for Oliva after you publicly named her."

"Why not? The story was wrong and she denied everything. He must have believed her."

"Let's assume for the moment that whether she was in on it or not, she's wasn't alone. She was doing it with or for someone else. Any thoughts on who that would be?"

"I've thought about that ever since the whole thing happened. Oliva was a politician who had power and was after more of it. Political power is a zero-sum game; if he had it, then that would mean someone else didn't. So there is no shortage of people who would benefit, or who would have a chance to benefit, from his falling on his ass."

"Or his death."

Bobby nods. "Or his death."

ndy, I need your okay on something. I want to call up the Bubeleh Brigade."

"Fine with me, Sam." The Bubeleh Brigade consists of Hilda and Eli Mandlebaum, Leon Goldberg, and Morris Fishman, each of them at least in their eighties. Sam taught a computer class for seniors at the Paterson YMHA, and they were his best students.

The Paterson YMHA, like the Paterson hospitals, is no longer in Paterson. It's in Wayne, along with William Paterson University, which used to be called Paterson State. I wonder how Willie P. would feel about his school not being in the city named after him.

It's just another indignity Paterson has suffered. I don't see New York University moving to Poughkeepsie, or the University of Chicago moving to Peoria. But it seems like everything in Paterson heads for the exits.

Except me.

Sam has called on the Bubeleh Brigade to work on a couple of cases for us in the past, and they are remarkably productive. Even more important is that Hilda makes the best rugelach and other baked goods in the history of the world. Hilda calls Sam *bubeleh,* which is how the group got its name.

"This cross-checking of the phone records is very time-consuming. With them I can get it done a lot faster."

"No problem, Sam."

"You sure?" Sam feels guilty when he can't immediately do these things by himself.

"I'm sure."

"It's just Hilda, Eli, and Leon. Unfortunately, Morris Fishman is no longer around."

"Dead?"

"Florida. Hilda told me he's the Phase Four shuffleboard champion."

I get off the phone and sit down for some light reading. The final toxicology report on the blood taken from Bobby has just come in. It shows a combination of fentanyl and alcohol, which I already knew, but one comment I find particularly interesting.

The toxicologist goes out of his way to say that the fentanyl amount in Bobby's system, especially when paired with the alcohol, "would in most cases be lethal."

If we take as a premise that some outside people did this to Bobby, then between the drug dose and the car crash, they may well have been trying to kill him. That is especially true since chances were good that the car would not have been discovered in the ditch for a long time; it was just a lucky break that it was found so soon.

So if my belief is that Bobby was set up and framed, the plan was probably supposed to culminate in his death. That makes sense because there would have been a much more cursory investigation by the police, and no pain-in-the-ass defense lawyer involved to look into it on Bobby's behalf.

Bobby's guilt would have been apparent to the police, they would have taken the obvious steps to confirm it, then moved on.

But Bobby lived, and here we are.

Laurie and I head out to the second murder scene, the one at Theresa Minardo's house. It's a quiet Clifton neighborhood, or at least it was quiet until her garage blew up.

The houses are fairly close together, which is why in addition to leveling the garage, the blast badly damaged both Theresa's house and the one next door. The garage is just a mound of rubble; nothing has been removed, and I don't know if Theresa has family that will step in and deal with this.

"According to the discovery, the bomb squad people say that the device was set off by the garage door opener, not the car," I say.

"I wonder exactly when she last put her car in the garage," Laurie says. "We know it was several days before the explosion, but we need to find out exactly when. I'll ask Corey to talk to the neighbors."

"Why is that important?"

"Because a lot of people with this setup, a long driveway leading up to the garage, don't bother putting it in all the time. They just let it sit in the driveway."

"Winter is different. Especially when it snows."

Laurie nods. "Exactly. If she put the car in the garage because the snow was coming that night, it would mean the device wasn't set yet. And if Theresa really stayed in the house because she was sick and also hiding from the press, then the device would have had to have been planted after the car was already in there. And while she was home."

"Very good point."

"I'll get Corey on that."

"I wonder if there was some kind of back door into the garage."

"Why?"

"Once Bobby was arrested, the press started showing up. They would have seen if somebody just opened the garage door. But they could have come in from the street behind here, if there was a way to get into the garage without being seen."

"Let's check a couple of other garages on the block. They all look the same."

We walk down the block and get a look at a couple of the garages. There's no back door, but there is a side door. Someone could have gotten in there without the media people seeing them, but there's no way to be sure.

With nothing else to learn, we head home. I hope we're done checking out murder scenes for a while.

Paterson's City Hall is an imposing building on Market Street in the downtown district.

Arriving at the building, one sees three statues. Two are of former mayors, Nathan Barnert and Andrew McBride, and one is of a former US vice president, Garret Hobart. The main thing that these three men have in common is that no one in Paterson has ever heard of them, although Barnert used to have a hospital named for him, back when Paterson had hospitals.

Other, more famous Patersonians seem to have been overlooked by the City Hall statue people. Lou Costello might have been a good choice, or Albert Sabin, who invented the oral polio vaccine. Or maybe Larry Doby, the second African American to reach the major leagues, and the first in the American League.

Personally, I would opt for Super Bowl–winning coach Bruce Arians or Giants wide receiver Victor Cruz. Or maybe Bruce Vilanch; if you've ever laughed at a joke watching the Academy Awards, the chances are that Bruce wrote it. He was also the center square on *Hollywood Squares,* which is even cooler than having a statue. Arians, Cruz, and Vilanch have all had at least some impact on my life; I certainly never sat down at the television to watch Garret Hobart.

The building itself is over a hundred years old and was modeled after the city hall in Lyon, France. Lyon was the silk center of Europe, and Paterson was at one time known as Silk City. These days you could walk around Paterson for a month and never see anyone draped in silk.

I'm here because Vince knows absolutely every politician in Paterson, and every one of them wants to get good coverage in Vince's newspaper. I wish Vince knew more defense attorneys, but unfortunately I seem to be his only connection to that world.

Vince has cleared the way for my meeting with Oscar Womack, the acting mayor. Womack had been head of the City Council, but moved into the big job on an interim basis when Tara dug up Mayor Oliva.

Womack had planned to run for mayor when Oliva ran for governor and was considered one of two favorites to win the position, the other being Police Commissioner Randy Bauer. So this is basically Womack getting a helpful head start, and this temporary incumbency can improve his chances, if he doesn't screw it up.

Womack keeps me waiting for twenty minutes before I am ushered into his office, but when I finally see him, he's smiling and happy. "Andy, good to see you again."

"Have we met before?"

He's distinctive looking, at least six feet tall and I'd guess well over 230 pounds, much of it in his stomach. He also has a thick black mustache. But I don't recall meeting him.

"Sure we did; sure we did. It was at the Boys and Girls Club Charity Dinner."

I have no recollection of it, though I seem to wind up at charity dinners fairly often. "Right. We both had the chicken."

He laughs. "I'm sure we did." He gestures for me to sit down in a leather chair opposite his desk.

"So you're the mayor."

He smiles sadly and gives an exaggerated shrug. "Somebody had to be." Then, "So tell me, how the hell did you wind up with Bobby Nash? I thought you prefer to win your cases. Wait, don't tell me . . . Vince."

"No, just my never-ending desire to see justice done."

"Believe me, I know what a pain Vince can be, especially lately. When I was on the City Council, the only way I could get my name in his paper would have been by taking an ad. Now that I'm the acting mayor, he gets on my case for every word I say."

"He's a fun guy."

"Yeah, tell me about it. You know, I liked Nash. He interviewed me a couple of times. Seemed like a good kid. I'm not saying he's guilty, that's up to the courts. But to do something like that . . ." Womack shakes his head.

"Oliva had a lot of enemies. Do you know anyone who would be happy he's dead?"

Another laugh; this is not a guy in deep mourning. "How much time do you have?"

Womack looks to the ceiling. "I'd better be careful; if there's anyone who would come back from the dead to get revenge, it's Alex. But, yes, Alex could be difficult to work with. Or talk with. Or exist with."

"Anyone specific?"

"You mean that might have killed him? Other than your client? I wouldn't think so. This is New Jersey, not the O.K. Corral."

"Did you know Theresa Minardo?"

"Sure. I wanted her to work for me; but she was going to ride Alex to Trenton. But at the end of the day she was a bit player. My guess, and I haven't really thought about this very much, is that whatever is going on, with your client or anyone else . . . she was collateral damage."

I don't say so, but that is my assessment as well. "What about Minchner?"

"You mean, do I think he could have slipped that money to Alex after all? Let's put it this way: when I first heard the story, I believed it. He's all about money, and he was on Alex's team. He must have been salivating when it looked like his boy could be governor; a million dollars would have been a small price to pay."

"You said 'when you first heard the story.'"

"Right. But then it didn't make a lot of sense. Minchner is smart, and so was Alex. They wouldn't have been so heavy-handed about it; they wouldn't have gotten caught. And once Nash said that Minardo was his source, the whole story fell apart. There is no way she would have turned on Alex. Not only did she believe in him, but he was her future meal ticket."

Womack looks at his watch. "Sorry, Andy, I have another meeting."

I think in this cell phone era the only reason that people wear watches is so that they can look at them as a way to justify ending meetings. "There's always another meeting," I say.

Just then the door opens and a young man comes in holding a piece of paper. "Excuse me. Sir, I think you'd want to see this."

He hands Womack the paper and he reads it quickly. "Damn. Now I've really got to go."

"Big news? Was Paterson just named Renaissance City of the Year?"

"I'm sure you'll read about it in Vince's paper tomorrow."

I'm not going to get any more information out of him, so I stand up to leave. "Thanks for seeing me. Do a good job and maybe you'll get a statue out front."

But he doesn't even answer; whatever just happened has his full attention.

ook how skinny you are. You're wasting away."

I've stopped in at Sam's office because he asked me to. He said that he and the Bubeleh Brigade have something to show me. Sam's office is right down the hall from mine, and this gives me an opportunity to drop my rent check off with Sofia Hernandez, my landlord and the owner of the building and the first-floor fruit stand below us.

Hilda Mandlebaum greets me with that concern about my weight before even saying hello. She adds, "Doesn't Laurie feed you?"

"Just some porridge, Hilda, and a few sips of water."

"We'll take care of that right now." She brings me over to Sam's desk, on which sits a tray of baked goods that Hilda obviously made herself and brought over. I can see four different flavors of rugelach.

"Perfect." I literally start to salivate. "This will teach Laurie a lesson; who is she to treat me like a street urchin?"

Once my mouth is stuffed, I stumble through some chitchat, getting reacquainted with Hilda, Eli, and Leon. They are as lively and animated as always; I hope I'm like that at their age. Actually, I wish I were like that at my age.

Finally, when I can't eat another bite, I turn to Sam.

"Let's hear what you've got; if I don't stop eating, I'm going to have to get my stomach pumped."

"Okay. We've finished our preliminary work on what phones were in the area of Theresa Minardo's house in that two-week period. There's not too much that was interesting."

"Yet you asked me to come down here."

"Right. I said 'not too much'; but there is something. The houses on that street are close together, and the GPS locaters are not exact. So some of the numbers could be phones that were actually next door, or just belonging to people hanging out on the street in front of her house."

"Got it."

"There are a total of fifty-one numbers."

"I'm surprised there are that many."

"Well, thirty-eight of them show up in one night, the first Saturday of the period we're talking about. I suspect either Theresa or one of her neighbors had a party."

"We can check that out."

"There is one number, though, that struck me as unusual. It's from the night of the mayor's murder, and it was at her house for two and a half minutes. That would eliminate a drive-by."

"What is it?"

"It's registered to a company called Elite Limousines. I don't know the name of the driver yet, but Leon is working on it."

"How can you get that?"

"I'm sure that Elite keeps their records on computer. If so, Leon can find it."

"Anything else?"

"Yes. It appears that they were dropping Theresa off. It was almost midnight, and we traced the phone back to the Hilton in the Meadowlands. After it was at Theresa's house, it went back to the Elite garage, in Garfield. The phone stayed in the car. We'll be able to confirm all this when Leon gets into the Elite computers."

"Did you check Theresa's phone?" I ask.

"Yes. She was at the hotel, and definitely in the limo. She arrived at the hotel at six thirty and stayed until eleven thirty, when she was driven home."

"I assume there's no way to know what she was doing there."

"Not from my end, no. You might be able to find out if there was some dinner or something, but we can't tell from here."

"Great, Sam. Keep me posted."

"Tell Laurie to feed you more," Hilda says.

I shake my head. "She won't listen; she's terribly mean." I say good-bye to all of them and ask Eli, who is Hilda's husband, how he managed to be married to her for fifty-four years without getting fat.

"All she gives me is porridge and a few sips of water," Eli says.

I head home, and the radio tells me what Acting Mayor Womack was reacting to when that note was brought in to him. The Paterson planning commissioner, Jason Civale, was arrested when cocaine and marijuana were found in his car during a routine traffic stop.

Civale is claiming that the drugs are not his and must have been planted there. For politicians, that is the drug version of "My Twitter account was hacked."

Womack, not wanting to look like his new administration is sordid or corrupt, even though Civale was an Oliva holdover, has already denounced Civale and appointed an interim replacement.

Never a dull moment in Paterson.

I've come to terms with the fact that I can't be absolutely sure my client is innocent.

My instinct is to believe him, but I am concerned that his phone was at Oliva's house and Eastside Park the night of the murder. I think that at the end of the day, meaning the end of our investigation, I'll know for sure one way or the other, so I have to wait.

But I absolutely do not believe that Bobby made up the story about the illegal contributions from Minchner to Oliva's campaign. It just doesn't make sense; the story could too easily have been disproven, as it was.

For Bobby to have faked it all, he would also have had to fabricate the canceled checks, and I just don't believe that he did that. He would have been playing with fire, risking his career, and it would have made no sense.

The incident itself no longer has any significance in the real world. It was shown to be false, and the target of it, Mayor Oliva, has now unceremoniously left the political scene. Bobby's journalism career is a thing of the past, and the lawsuits against the newspaper have been withdrawn.

But for me, and for our defense, it is still of great importance. If Bobby did not make up that story and fabricate that evidence, then someone else did. That someone else was trying to sandbag Oliva's career; even if the story was subsequently shown to be false, it still could have tainted him for the governor's race.

I doubt Bobby was the one they were after; I suspect he was simply the vehicle they were using to get at Oliva. He may well have been chosen because of his relative inexperience and his obvious ambition; they played him for a sucker.

If Oliva was the target, if an elaborate effort was made to damage him politically, then it didn't work. He used it to play the victim card, and to attack the press. If anything, his deft handling of it helped him politically.

But once that didn't work, then whoever tried it took more significant action. They removed Oliva from the political scene, and from every other scene, permanently. The overriding point is that he had a serious enemy, other than Bobby. If we can identify that enemy for the jury, exposing him or them as a threat, then they might find reasonable doubt as to Bobby's guilt.

I've believed from the beginning that Oliva was the main target, and that Theresa Minardo was possibly killed simply to build more of a case against Bobby. While I still consider that to be the case, it doesn't mean she is not an important player here, because she is.

Theresa Minardo pulled Bobby in with information about Oliva, and she provided him with the faked checks, though she sent them in an envelope that couldn't be traced back to her.

It would have made no sense for Bobby to make up her involvement; she could too easily deny it. I doubt that she did it alone, so she must have dealt with the people that were trying to damage Oliva. They must have given her the checks.

On the surface, her involvement as the source of the story makes little sense. Once I get under the surface, it makes even less sense. By all accounts she was a big fan of Oliva's, and she certainly had a lot to gain by his political ascension. So why would she have tried to make him look corrupt?

Maybe she was a secret enemy of Oliva's as well, even though she worked for him and professed her allegiance. Once she was caught, she backtracked, but that wouldn't necessarily negate her original intention. But her turning on him flies in the face of everything I have heard about her.

One thing is for sure: she knew who Oliva's enemies were, and she died with that knowledge. She might well have died *because* of that knowledge.

I have no idea if Minardo's visit to the hotel that night was in any way sinister or related to our case. There are many ways in which it could have been innocent: she could have been having dinner with colleagues, or visiting with a friend in from out of town.

But I was at her house; I saw where she lived. It was not an area that would be described as upscale. It would not be commonplace for people living in that neighborhood to be taking limousines; not when they had a car sitting in their driveway or their garage.

Thinking about that reminds me to call Corey Douglas and ask what he found out from Theresa's neighbors about her habits regarding where she parked her car.

"It was almost always in the driveway," Corey says. "It's never on the street because the spots are limited and they're very hard to get. The neighbors said that if it was in the garage, it was probably because of the predicted snow. I talked to the person who did her plowing for her, and he confirmed it. He said she always put it in the garage when a snowstorm was coming."

I brief Corey on what Sam learned about the limo. "Maybe she needed to go to the hotel, but didn't want to drive in case the snow started early," I say.

"I don't buy it. Someone like that, someone like me in fact, if you can't drive or don't want to, you call a cab or an Uber. Not a limo."

"You're probably right."

"Did she go to the hotel in a limo as well?" Corey asks. "And if so, where did they pick her up?"

"I don't know the answer to those questions, but I'm sure Sam will find out."

When I get off that call, I place one to Sam, just to make sure he's checking on the things Corey is talking about.

"Come on, Andy, you really think you have to tell me that?"

"Actually, I don't. But there's one other thing."

"What's that?"

"Theresa's garage could easily be approached from the street behind it. Can you add that street, in the area adjacent to the garage, to your phone check?"

"If they brought their phone with them to the garage, it would have already shown up on what we've done so far."

"I understand that, but they could have left their phone in the car. They might even have anticipated that some-body, probably the police, could be checking the GPSs like we are."

"Good point."

"Put one of your top elderly Jewish computer people on it."

He laughs. "I will. Eli Mandlebaum will be perfect for the job."

The explosion went off at 11:38 P.M. in the Broadway Bus Terminal in Paterson.

Because of the lateness of the hour, and because the last buses leaving or arriving for the night had long ago finished their work, there was only one injury.

A maintenance man, Ronald Phelan of Haledon, sustained non-life-threatening injuries. He was unquestionably lucky; he was in the bathroom in the section of the building farthest from the explosion.

Had he been doing his ordinary rounds, emptying trash cans throughout the building, he would most likely have been killed.

The police and bomb squad arrived on the scene within minutes of the explosion, and at least in the early hours of the investigation had no suspect.

The only clue as to the perpetrators was a handwritten note pasted on the front door of the bus terminal that read BE READY.

While everyone in Paterson is talking about the explosion at the bus terminal, our house has a different focus.

Today is wrapping day.

One of the charity things we do during the holiday season is to buy gifts for people that we don't know. Our local post office has a small Christmas tree, and people who can't afford to buy gifts put little cards on the tree. They contain their wish lists, usually for their kids.

Laurie and I take a whole bunch of the cards, buy the gifts, and ship them to the families. We do it anonymously, and it's one of the things about Christmas that I like.

Most of the stores we buy the gifts at offer to wrap them, but Laurie acts as if they've offered her a jug full of pestilence. Laurie prefers to wrap them herself.

And I'm not talking about ordinary wrapping. Laurie is the Picasso of gift wrappers. Each wrapping is a work of art, topped off by twirly ribbons. Only when the packages are perfect will she ship them off, so that some eager kid somewhere can rip off the wrapping without even looking at it.

Needless to say, I do not participate in the wrapping, nor is my help in any way solicited. Ricky acts as Laurie's trusted assistant, handing her ribbon or scissors or tape or whatever else she needs. I used to do the job, but traitor Ricky has usurped my position in an obvious attempt to curry favor with Laurie.

Now I'm going to have to find a new way to curry favor with Laurie, which is a problem, because my favor-currying skills are decidedly limited.

With nothing else to do, I place my third call to Richard Minchner, and for the third time I reach his assistant, James Pritchett. The word *assistant* is vague. It could mean that the person effectively runs the boss's life, or it could mean that the person's main function is to get coffee on command, or maybe to hand the boss ribbon or scissors on wrapping day.

I get the feeling that Pritchett leans more toward the life-running type of assistant because he sounds confident when he tells me that Minchner is way too busy to see me. I have no idea if Pritchett is telling me the truth, or if Minchner is just blowing me off. I don't even know if Pritchett has shared with him that I am making these calls.

"I told you, we will call you when and if Mr. Minchner decides to speak with you."

"I'm surprised he's not anxious to meet me. I'm a very personable guy."

"You're also representing a murderer and a man who wrongly tried to implicate Mr. Minchner in a criminal conspiracy."

"Reasonable people can disagree with that assessment. But here's a fact that no one can disagree with. Your boss will talk to me and he will answer my questions. He can do it in his office or he can do it in court in front of a judge and a court reporter. So if you are a competent assistant, and I have no doubt that you are, you will make him understand that."

Pritchett seems less than fully impressed by my speech and blows me off again. With no one willing to talk to me and my wrapping services not required, I take Tara and Hunter down to the Tara Foundation. I don't bring Sebastian since he always makes it obvious that he would rather sleep.

Tara and Hunter like playing with the dogs awaiting adoption at the foundation, so Willie and Sondra let them all out into the center of the play area. Tara plays for about a half hour, after which she is always so exhausted that she can barely make it back into the car.

"How is Vince doing with Duchess?" Sondra asks.

"I think it's going to be a long haul," I say. "What did you think?"

"Hard to say; she is really adorable. Maybe she'll win his heart."

"Funny, I never thought of Vince as having a heart. I'd have to see an ultrasound before I'd believe it."

Willie asks me if I've heard about the explosion in the bus station last night, and I tell him that of course I have. He asks if it's possibly related to the explosion that killed Theresa Minardo.

"Unfortunately, I doubt it," I say.

"Why unfortunately?"

"Because Bobby couldn't have set this one off."

My cell phone rings and I see from the caller ID that it is James Pritchett, Minchner's assistant. "Mr. Minchner will give you fifteen minutes."

This guy is on my nerves. "Not enough time. I like to

chitchat for at least ten minutes when I first meet someone to break the ice. It takes at least that long for my charm to kick in."

"You are an annoying man, Mr. Carpenter."

"So I've been told. When does he want to meet?"

"I'm not sure I'd phrase it that way. Mr. Minchner will *consent* to meet in forty-five minutes at his office."

"You're pretty annoying yourself, Mr. Pritchett. And this barely gives me enough time to get my hair done first."

"Shall I put you on his calendar, or not?"

"I'll be there."

I get off the phone and turn to Sondra. "Someone just told me that I am annoying."

She smiles. "Hard to imagine."

"Can I pick up Tara and Hunter when I get back?"

She looks toward the center of the floor, where Tara and Hunter are rolling around happily with their friends. "They'll be out cold by then."

I'm on the way to Minchner's office when the phone rings; it's Sam. "Eli strikes again. You're gonna like this."

Another prediction from Sam, this one more promising. "I'm looking forward to hearing it."

"Elite Limousines picked up Theresa Minardo at her house that night. Either the driver didn't have his phone with him then, or it was shut off, because the GPS hadn't shown up in the records.

"They sent a sedan, not a stretch limo, so I would think that it would have drawn less attention. It took her to the Hilton, and drove her home at eleven thirty."

There's not much new here, so I'm waiting for Sam to get to the main point.

Which he does. "The limo was reserved by a company called Tri-Tex. They are a shipping company, mostly handling textiles. But get this: they're one of a bunch of companies owned by RMD Enterprises, which in turn is seventy percent owned by none other than Richard Minchner."

"Any chance Minchner had a room reserved at the hotel?"

"No, but Tri-Tex did."

"What does the *D* stand for?"

"What do you mean?"

"*RMD.* Richard Minchner covers the *R* and *M.* What about the *D*?"

"I have no idea."

"Once again, you and Leon have let me down. But you can make up for it. Get me the name and address for the guy who drove her."

For a guy who owns so many companies, Richard Minchner has a surprisingly small office.

RMD Enterprises occupies only one floor of a three-story office building in Secaucus. It's just a couple of minutes from the Meadowlands, so if Minchner or one of his people met Theresa Minardo at the Hilton, it was convenient.

The office list in the lobby mentions only eleven people as working here for RMD. James Pritchett, who referred to himself as Minchner's assistant, is listed as a senior vice president. I'd better keep this news from Edna, or she might start referring to herself as emperor of Andy Carpenter Enterprises.

I take the elevator up, and it opens not into a hallway but into the reception area for RMD. Nothing about the offices is particularly striking; the furnishings are bland and fairly conservative. Minchner, for all his money, must not be a flashy guy.

I tell the receptionist my name, and within moments a man in his midthirties, tall and impeccably dressed, comes out. Chances are good that his suit cost more than my entire wardrobe, which isn't saying much. I wouldn't even own a suit if I didn't need one when I go to court, which represents another in an endless list of good reasons to retire.

He introduces himself as James Pritchett but makes no effort to shake hands. That'll teach me a lesson. "Mr. Carpenter. Right this way, if you please."

He said "if you please" in an annoying, condescending tone. I wonder which way he'd want me to go if I didn't please, but I don't bother asking. Instead I just follow him through the door and down the hall to Minchner's office.

When the door opens, Minchner is at his desk pretending to be working. He looks up as if surprised to be interrupted, even though he would undoubtedly know I was being brought back this way, if I pleased.

"Carpenter," he says.

"Minchner," I say.

"Sit down."

"Okay." Then I turn to Pritchett. "See? This is what I meant by starting the meeting with some chitchat."

"Thank you, James," Minchner says, which is as clearly a directive for Pritchett to leave the room as if Minchner had said, *Get the hell out of my office, James.*

Pritchett leaves.

"I know that crap about everyone being entitled to a defense, but—"

I interrupt, "You mean that constitutional crap?"

"Yeah. But I still don't see how you can represent that guy."

"Damn . . . I should have checked with you first, but now it's too late."

"Ask your questions."

"First one. Whoever faked those checks and gave them to Bobby Nash—"

"Nash did it on his own. He thought it would make him a star."

"Whoever did it . . . why do you think they picked you?"

"I don't know; maybe he knew I have a lot of money and I share it with candidates I support. But it was stupid, because if he knew anything about me, he would know that I'd fight back and clear my name."

"Is Alex Oliva one of the candidates you supported?"

Minchner nods. "One of them. It's all in the public record."

"You're active in New Jersey politics. Who stands to benefit from Oliva's death?"

"Your reputation is that you're a smart guy, in addition to being an asshole. Why are you asking me such an obvious question?"

"To hear your answer."

"Aaron Widener. He's now going to be the next governor of New Jersey, but Oliva would have cleaned his clock in the primaries."

That confirms the view I've heard from other people, including Vince. Widener is widely considered to be the new favorite for the governorship.

"Did you know Theresa Minardo?"

"I'm sure I met her at some point, but I don't recall it specifically."

"When was the last time you saw her?"

"I just told you I don't remember."

"Let me try and refresh your memory. Did you meet her at the Hilton?"

I said that to see what reaction I would get, and I get anger. I was hoping for fear, or at least concern. "What the hell does that mean?"

"Which part of the question didn't you understand?"

"This interview is over, Mr. Carpenter. You need someone to show you out?"

"No, I just make a left and go down the hall, if I please."

My experience at RMD was not pleasant. I do not like Richard Minchner or James Pritchett, but the receptionist seemed okay, in a perky, irritating sort of way.

It's possible that I did not like them because of their obvious hostility toward me. On one level their hostility could make sense, despite my obvious charm and affability. If Minchner was an innocent victim of the Bobby Nash story, a big if, then they could see him as an enemy.

As someone probably once said, "The lawyer of my enemy is my enemy."

The unfortunate truth is that the people who planted the fake story about Alex Oliva weren't necessarily involved in his death.

I've been operating on the assumption that they were, since they were obviously Oliva's enemies and because Theresa Minardo is the common thread running through both Bobby's story and the recent murders.

But Oliva, because of his position and his likely future in Trenton, most certainly had other enemies who could have had their own motives for killing him. And in their planning, they could have sat back, surveyed the scene, and looked for a likely person to blame.

Bobby would have fit that bill, and that could be why Theresa Minardo was killed as well. She could have been an innocent bystander, but the killers would have known that her death made it easier to pin Oliva's death on Bobby. He had a public grudge against both of them; in his mind Oliva and Minardo had led to his public humiliation and cost him his career.

In terms of an investigation leading to a successful defense, we have a significantly better chance if the people behind the story are in fact the killers. We can more easily home in on that area, and the main advantage is that Theresa Minardo represents avenues to pursue.

If the killers are unrelated to Bobby's story and had other reasons for wanting Oliva dead, the whole case becomes much more open-ended and much less manageable for us. Then we're left with the daunting task of identifying Oliva's enemies and trying to figure out which ones might have violently removed him.

When faced with a dilemma like this, one that requires clear thinking and decisive strategizing, I do what I always do: I walk the dogs. The peacefulness and solitude, interrupted only occasionally by leaning over with the dreaded plastic bag, is conducive to sober reflection.

Tara is my sounding board. I speak to her about my problems and challenges, and her responses are always perfect. She never talks back to me and never tells me I'm wrong or an idiot. Instead she listens silently and sympathetically and even throws in an occasional tail wag in support.

"You started it, you know," I say to Tara. "You dug the guy up in the first place."

She doesn't respond for two reasons. For one thing, she's a dog. For another, she knows that I'm just venting and know better. Once the snow melted, Oliva's body would have been found and Vince would still have called me. All Tara did was speed the process along.

Besides, she's a golden retriever. There's not a golden retriever on the planet who wouldn't have been curious about whatever she thought might have been buried in that snow. She expected a squirrel and instead got a mayor. It could happen to anyone.

Hunter also wanted to go over there that night with

Tara, though he could just have been following her. Sebastian wasn't interested; the only things he would have bothered to dig up would be either a hamburger or a recliner lounge or a dog hammock.

In terms of thinking about case strategy, it's an unproductive walk. The best I can come up with is not to eliminate either approach; I'm going to focus on whoever was behind Bobby's bogus story, but also look into other enemies Oliva might have had.

I'm heading back when my cell phone rings. It's Laurie, asking me when I'll be home.

"I'm on the way now. The timing is dependent on how fast Sebastian is willing to move his stubby legs."

"Okay. Good. Because we might have something for you."

T his is Roger Parker," Laurie says. "Roger . . . Andy Carpenter."

I knew that Laurie said she had something for me, but I didn't realize it was an actual person waiting in our den.

He is an African American with graying hair at the sides, tall, but it's hard to estimate his height because he has immediately bent over to pet our three dogs. My kind of guy.

We say our hellos, and Laurie says that Corey had spoken with Roger at his home. When Corey told him that I would want to speak with him as well, he said that he would stop by, because he works at a car dealership not far from here, just off Route 20. Corey is not here as well because he is still out talking to other neighbors of Roger's.

"What are we going to talk about?" I ask.

"Mr. Parker lives on the street behind Theresa Minardo's house. Actually, his house is right behind hers, so their garages sit back-to-back."

He frowns. "Her garage is not there anymore; and mine is not currently usable."

"Did you know her?" I ask.

"Not really. I talked to her a few times when we both happened to be in our backyards, but it was mostly small talk. The weather, that kind of thing. She seemed like a nice lady."

"Tell Andy about the night that it snowed," Laurie says.

Parker nods. "Well, this was before the snow, although it was predicted to start later that night. It was about eight o'clock, and I was coming home from work. My plan was to put the car in the garage, because of the weather forecast. That's pretty much the only time I put my car inside it.

"Anyway, when I got home, there was a car blocking my driveway. There are rarely any parking spots available on our street. There are a lot of two-family homes, so there are just more people and cars than available spots. But this driver didn't seem to care about that because he just blocked my driveway. It was really annoying; I was tired and didn't want to have to deal with it."

"What did you do?"

"Well, I parked in a neighbor's driveway. He was standing outside, and I told him it was just until I could get rid of the other car. He was fine with it. Then I went in my house and called the police. They didn't seem impressed, but they said they would send a car out when they had someone available.

"I went back outside in case the driver was around. I didn't see anybody, and I didn't know when the cops would come, so I took a picture of the license plate. I didn't know what good it would do, but I wanted to have it to show them if they came after the car was gone. It was a rental car." He shows us the picture of the plate, and I write down the number.

"How do you know that?" Laurie asks.

"It had that kind of E-ZPass thing on the windshield

that flips open; it's the kind that rental car companies use. Anyway, I went in the house and looked outside about ten minutes later and the car was gone. So I got my car from the neighbor's driveway and moved it into my garage."

"Did the police ever show up?"

Parker nods. "They did, about twenty minutes later. The cop was annoyed that I hadn't called them back to say that the car was gone, but I forgot."

"Did you get the cop's name?"

"No."

"Did you show them the photo?"

"No, it didn't seem to matter at that point, and it's not like they were going to hunt him down for illegal parking."

Laurie asks, "So you have no idea how long he was there; you just know how long he was there after you got home?"

Parker nods. "That's right. Could that car have had something to do with the murder?"

"It's possible," I say. "I should tell you that you might be called in to court to testify to all of this."

"Will it take much time? My work—"

"I'd make sure it was quick. That I can promise."

Parker smiles. "Then I'm happy to help. Whoever did that . . ." He doesn't finish his sentence . . . he doesn't have to.

Parker gives the dogs a few more pets, which they accept quite willingly, then leaves.

Once he's gone, I call Sam. "Sam, there was a car parked on the street right behind Theresa Minardo's house around eight P.M. on the night the mayor was killed. I don't know what time it got there, but it was there for at least ten minutes, maybe longer, and it was gone by around eight fifteen. Can you see if any phone GPS information matches that?"

"Sure."

"Also, the license plate on the car was MCT384. It was a Massachusetts plate and might have been rented. Can you track that down?"

"You got it. And I got you the name and address of the limo driver."

"Great." I write down the information and then get off the phone.

Laurie asks, "You think it means something?"

"The only thing that gives me hope is that it happened while Theresa Minardo was at the hotel. Maybe she was brought there at least partially to get her out of the house so the explosive could be planted."

"So we wait for Sam."

I nod. "Shouldn't take long; he'll probably put the Mandlebaums on it. They're like senior Jewish pit bulls."

They're planning to move me to the jail tomorrow," Bobby says when he calls.

"Okay. I'll get Eddie to file a motion asking the judge to delay it, but it's a long shot." Judges tend to want to move control of the accused from the police to the Department of Corrections, mostly for budgetary reasons. "How are you feeling?"

"Pretty good."

"Well, start moaning a lot, just for effect."

I hang up and head for my next meeting, with the limo driver, Carl McKenzie. I call Eddie on the way to ask him to file the motion. "The judge will probably tackle this for a loss," he says, calling on his apparently endless supply of sports references.

As I'm reaching the door of the Suburban Diner in Paramus, a middle-aged man is already entering. He's wearing a black suit and dark blue tie. The suit is a little glossy looking and screams *limo driver*.

"Mr. McKenzie?"

He turns around and smiles. "Mr. Carpenter?"

"That's me. Let's grab a table."

We sit down and each order coffee. He gets a toasted bagel and I get a fruit cup. I'm still conscious of the four million calories' worth of rugelach that I inhaled the other day, and I'm also planning to have some more the next time I go to Sam's office. And I am definitely planning to find some excuse to go to Sam's office, as soon as I'm sure that more rugelach has entered the building.

I tell McKenzie the specific date I'm talking about. "You picked up a woman named Theresa Minardo at her house."

He hesitates. "I'm not sure what I can say. Company policy is to maintain the privacy of our clients."

"Mr. McKenzie, I'm a lawyer, and any lawyer will tell you that there is no such thing as limo driver–client privilege. You're going to have to answer these questions, either here at the Suburban Diner over coffee or in court without coffee."

"I understand, but—"

"You know Ms. Minardo was murdered, right?"

"I know."

"Then you know this is important. So let's start again. You picked her up at her house and you took her to the Hilton."

He nods. "Right."

"Was she alone?"

"Yes."

"Was that the first time you drove her anywhere?"

"No, I drove her quite a few times before. Always to that hotel."

"When you took her home, was she alone?"

"Yes."

"Her being alone . . . was that true the other times you drove her as well?"

"Yes."

He seems uncomfortable, but at least he's answering

the questions. "Do you know the purpose of her visits to the hotel?"

"No." Then, "But I think she was meeting a man."

"What makes you say that?"

"Sometimes she would make a phone call. We were always in a sedan, so I could hear her. I wasn't trying to eavesdrop, but I couldn't help it."

"What was the nature of the calls?"

"Just to say that she was on her way, that kind of thing. But the way she talked made me think she was meeting a man. Just a feeling I had."

"Did she arrange for the cars herself?"

"I don't think so. I think it was done for her, but I don't know by who."

I don't push that because I can find out through the company. "On the night we are talking about, did she make any phone calls?"

He hesitates. "Yes. She called to say that she would be there in a few minutes, and that she was looking forward to it."

"Anything else?"

"Yes. She asked what was the room number, and she repeated it after she heard it."

"Do you remember the room number?"

"Yes. Nine fourteen."

"How do you happen to remember that?"

"September fourteenth is my birthday."

The room number was the guy's birthday. I don't usually get this lucky; hopefully it's the start of a trend.

As hard to believe as it seems, Christmas has crept up on me. I'm actually surprised that it's here.

One of the reasons that is so remarkable is that I spend all day every day listening to Bing Crosby telling me that "it's Christmastime in the city." Today, the one day it is actually Christmastime in the city, I forgot about it; although fortunately I did remember to buy presents for Laurie and Ricky a few weeks ago.

And by the way, do silver bells sound different from other bells?

But I can tell the big day is here because Ricky wakes us up at five thirty to ask what time it is. Before long we're all up and opening gifts that Laurie has wrapped and placed under the tree.

I get the same thing I get for every occasion, and the only thing I ever want . . . chocolate-covered cherries.

Ricky gets a bunch of stuff. He's into music now, and not the Bing Crosby kind. One of the things he asked Laurie to get him is a download of music by a band called Garbage.

I admit I've never heard of them, so they may or may not live up to their billing. They've apparently been around a long time and are successful, but I can't help picturing the meeting they must have had to come up with the name for their band.

We need to find something that appeals to people and at the same time says that we create quality music, one of them probably said. *A name that will stand the test of time and span generations.*

I've got it, said another. *Garbage! It's already in every house in the country . . . the world. And it will be around forever . . . it's not going away, it's actually piling up! We can ride the wave.*

The music that Ricky asked for is their greatest hits album. It's called, naturally, *Absolute Garbage*.

But despite the concerns that this raises about Ricky's mental health, Christmas is a really good day. Not Thanksgiving good, but a respectable second. It's not usually a football day, but the NBA always schedules five games that include their best matchups. If they're going to go to that kind of trouble, then the least I can do is watch them.

We always have our Christmas meal at around two o'clock. I'm not sure if it's lunch or dinner, and it makes adjusting my eating for the rest of the day a challenge, but I'm not complaining. Laurie always makes a great meal, and if I get hungry later, I have all those chocolate-covered cherries.

We've just finished eating when Sam calls. "We've got some information for you. You're going to like it."

"Sam, you're working on Christmas?"

"Andy, my team consists of Leon Goldberg and the Mandlebaums. We take Purim off."

"I don't know what I was thinking. What have you got?"

"So it turns out there was a phone on the street behind

the Minardo house at that time. It was there for ten minutes. The phone is registered to a Drew Churasick.

"The car with that license plate you gave me was in fact a rental car. It was rented at Newark Airport and returned there the next day. The renter of the car was Ronald Devers. Devers flew the next day to Detroit."

"So the phone guy and the car guy are two different people?"

"I don't think so," Sam says. "As far as Hilda can determine, and Hilda can determine really far, Devers doesn't exist. We have his driver's license and credit card information from the rental, and it's all fake."

"What about the Churasick name?"

"That seems to be real. There is a Drew Churasick that lives in Detroit, and the address we have matches the phone records."

"Do you know anything about him?"

"He's former Special Forces; served in Iraq. For three years he worked as a security consultant for a company called Martel."

"I never heard of it."

"You really only have to know one thing, and it's courtesy of Leon Goldberg. Martel is owned by RMD Enterprises, which in turn is owned by Richard Minchner."

"Merry Christmas to me. Thanks, Sam."

"Don't thank me; it's all the Bubeleh Brigade. They're unbelievable."

"That's for sure. When it's all over, we'll have a party; Hilda can do the baking."

I get off and tell Laurie the new revelation, and she

shares my view that this is the first real example of major progress. There is zero possibility that an employee of Richard Minchner's was just coincidentally visiting on that particular night someone who lived behind Theresa Minardo.

The question now is what to do with this information. It's important enough that it takes my attention away from the Celtics-Bucks game.

But it's not important enough to keep the dogs from wanting to be walked, so I head out to do that. I make it a short one, about twenty minutes, but I have to promise them that we'll do a long one tomorrow.

When I get back, Laurie is waiting for me on the front porch. It's cold and she's not wearing a coat, so it must be important.

"What's wrong?"

"You need to get out to the hospital."

"Why?"

"Something happened to Bobby."

Three police cars are in front of the hospital when I arrive.

None of the cops are downstairs, so there is no one for me to ask what is going on. Not that they would tell me anyway.

I head up to Bobby's floor, and there doesn't seem to be an increased level of activity. I don't stop at the nurses' station; instead I go down the hall toward the room.

At least a half dozen cops are milling around, and I ask one what is going on.

"Who are you?" he asks.

"I'm Bobby Nash's lawyer."

Another cop says, "He's Andy Carpenter."

"Well, now that we have that cleared up," I say, "will you tell me what the hell is going on?"

"Your client has a problem."

This cop is annoying me to the point where I might punch him, and then I'd have a problem. So instead I walk by them and head for the door.

"He ain't in there," a cop says.

"Where is he?"

"Mr. Carpenter, perhaps you should come with me." It's one of the nurses that I met in a previous visit.

She sounds like the voice of reason, so I follow her to a small waiting room. She closes the door behind her.

She doesn't waste any time. "Mr. Nash has been taken to surgery; he might be in intensive care by now."

"What happened?"

"He became violently ill and his organs started to shut down. He went into a coma."

"Is he going to survive?"

"I'm afraid I don't know the answer to that. I do know that the doctors were extremely concerned. He's in excellent hands."

"What caused it?"

"That's hard to say; I can only speculate."

"Speculation would be welcome at this point."

She looks around the empty room as if to determine that we're not being overheard. "I think he was poisoned. This happened shortly after his meal, and I can't think of another explanation. I've never seen a reaction like that, but of course I'm not his doctor, and I haven't seen his test results, so I hope I'm wrong."

I thank her for talking to me about this. I don't know yet if I hope she's wrong in her diagnosis; I just want whatever is the matter with Bobby to be something he can recover from.

It's two more hours until I hear from the doctor. "It's going to be at least twenty-four hours until we know which way this is going to go."

"Are you optimistic?"

He shrugs. "I'm an optimistic person, so maybe fifty-fifty? It's lucky this happened to him here. We were able to treat him immediately. If he had had to be transported to a hospital, he never would have made it."

"What happened to him?"

"Sorry . . . I assumed you knew. He was poisoned."

"Do you know how it happened?"

"He ingested it with his food. I don't know how it got in there, but I imagine there will be a very significant investigation. I do know that our kitchen has been closed and probably will be for a while."

"Were the police not outside his room when the food came in?"

"That doesn't seem to have been the problem; somehow whoever did this infiltrated the kitchen. It came up and into the room as it normally does. The police would have had no reason to suspect anything."

There's no sense hanging around here anymore. I leave word with the nurses to call me if there are any developments, and I head home. On the way I call Eddie Dowd and tell him not to bother filing the motion to keep Eddie in the hospital.

Someone else has taken care of that for us.

When I get home, I fill Laurie in on the news from the hospital. After I do so, I say, "This has implications for our case."

She nods her understanding. "That's for sure. It's no easy thing to have accomplished; if someone managed to poison Bobby in a hospital, they likely did so for more than revenge, or even hate. And they are good at what they do."

"Right. And they would think that killing him ends any more need for an investigation."

She smiles. "They don't know you or us very well."

"No, they don't."

f Laurie and I are right that the motive for poisoning Bobby is to stop our investigation, then the killers of Oliva and Theresa Minardo have to be behind it.

They are the only ones threatened by the investigation's continuing, even though we are not at a stage where we are a threat to anyone. Knowing this doesn't get us any closer to figuring out who it is, but it does go a long way to getting us to believe that they are out there.

Bobby did not poison himself.

If Minchner is behind this, and I am a long way from being anywhere close to sure that is the case, then I may have precipitated the attempt on Bobby's life.

When I met with him, I indirectly but clearly confronted him with my knowledge of Theresa Minardo's going to the Hilton that night. I was just doing it to get a reaction, to rattle his cage and see how he reacted, but it might have triggered an overreaction, which in turn has Bobby in intensive care.

Vince calls, and the first words out of his mouth are "He's going to make it."

"Did you talk to him?"

"No, he's still out of it. But I talked to the doctors. It might take a while, but he'll come all the way back."

"Vince, I need you to find out what you can about Richard Minchner."

"What are you looking for?"

"I don't know, but you're tied into ways to get information on him that we could never top. I want to know what your reporters think, not just what they can print. Include your business reporters; I want to know what makes his company tick. But talk to everyone—people at other newspapers; call in favors. I want to fully understand Minchner."

"You think he could be the bad guy here?"

I don't want to tell Vince too much; I want to be the receiver of information, not the provider. "I don't know; but it is definitely a box worth checking."

"Okay. I assume this is a rush?"

"You assume correctly. And, Vince, don't keep it quiet. I want everyone to know you are asking, and very specifically asking for me."

"Okay. You want to tell me why?"

The answer, which I will not tell Vince, is that if Minchner has something to be afraid of, I want to force him into a mistake. Thinking that getting rid of Bobby will leave him in the clear is an example of what I consider a mistake.

I decide to just ignore the question; Vince is smart enough to know what that means. "How's Duchess doing?"

"Duchess? Not bad."

This represents a major change in attitude. "Really? She growing on you?"

"We're working it out."

"No more shitting on the floor?"

"I said we're working it out. You want me to get started on this Minchner thing or not?"

"Bye, Vince." Then, "Oh, one more thing. Can you get me in to see Aaron Widener?" Widener is the man who all experts feel has the inside track on the governorship, now that Oliva is permanently out of the picture.

"Another favor?"

"Vince, how'd you like to start defending Bobby Nash by yourself? And make sure he can pay your fee, because you're going to be buying your own beer and burgers."

"Okay, it was a joke. I know Widener, son of a bitch that he is. I'll see what I can do."

I get off the phone just as Laurie is coming into the room.

"That was Vince. Bobby is going to make it."

"Fantastic."

"And he didn't say so, but I think Duchess may be growing on him."

She nods. "I'm telling you. Down deep in Vince there is a normal human being. He cares about Bobby, he's starting to like having a dog, it's all starting to come out. Next thing you know he'll be crying at sappy commercials and going to Meryl Streep movies."

"It's disorienting. Vince being an ice-cold pain in the ass is something I felt I could hold on to. The world is changing and I might not be ready for it."

I almost never call team meetings except for the one at the start of a case, but this situation calls for it.

A lot is going on and I have assignments to give out. I also want to make sure that we are on the same page. During the pretrial phase the cracks that things can slip through are a mile wide.

This time we're doing it at our house, mainly because meeting here is more comfortable than in the cramped office.

The other positive to having the meeting here is that Corey brings Simon Garfunkel, his German shepherd and former police partner in the K-9 squad. Simon sometimes attends meetings in my office as well, but here he gets to play with his best friend, Tara. Hunter also tries to get involved in the wrestling, while Sebastian finds the whole concept of movement to be annoying and beneath him.

Tonight is New Year's Eve, a holiday that has absolutely no significance for Laurie and me. It's been a while since the big night has seen us go out; now it's a struggle just to stay up until midnight to watch the ball drop. It's a struggle we've lost the last three years, by an increasing amount of time each year.

So I have everyone gathered here. We're sitting in our

living room, not at a conference table, but rather spread out on couches and chairs. Edna does not have a table to take notes on, which is not a problem because Edna does not take notes. I'm not sure I've ever seen her with a pen; she uses pencils for her crossword puzzles.

I debated having the Bubeleh Brigade join the meeting, but ultimately decided it wasn't necessary. Sam can fill them in on whatever they need to know, and I don't want to interfere with their work or with Hilda's baking.

I update everyone on all that has gone on so far, including Bobby's condition. The news on that front is getting more positive; he is a lucky guy for someone who has been extraordinarily unlucky.

"Let's start with Bobby," I say. "He's going to be in the hospital for a while. Based on what happened, that means he's in some danger. I'm not worried about somebody breaking into his room; the police presence there has been increased. But I am worried about another attempt like the last one."

"Have they figured out how it happened?" Corey asks.

"No, which means it could happen again. Laurie, you, Corey, and Marcus can divide this up however you want, but you need to work with the hospital and the cops to make sure that Bobby is safe.

"Pulling off what they already did in the hospital shows that we are dealing with powerful and resourceful people. We have to respond in kind."

I turn to Corey and Marcus. "One of you should start tailing Richard Minchner. Do a bad job of it and make sure he knows what you're doing. Once he's onto you, you can back off most of the time; he'll just think you're there but he doesn't see you. I want him worried; maybe he will panic and make a mistake."

"Or maybe he'll decide the best move is not to kill Bobby but to kill you," Laurie says.

"I can take care of myself."

"Andy . . . ," Laurie starts.

"I thought I could slip that one past you. Sam, your team has a lot to do. But don't overwork them; I don't know if you noticed, but they're not getting any younger. Give them New Year's Day off."

"It's not their New Year, Andy."

"You sure about that?"

"Pretty sure. They've had like five thousand of them already."

"I just thought maybe they celebrate this New Year also, but, okay, turn your place into a senior-Hebrew sweatshop. Either way, I want you to do a cyber rectal exam on Minchner; find out everything you can about his company. I have Vince doing the noncyber version."

"Okay."

"Also, and this might be urgent, I want you to focus on Drew Churasick, the guy who parked behind Theresa Minardo's house that night. I especially want to know if he is back in this area. That would make him a suspect for the incident at the hospital."

"You got it," Sam says.

"And see if you can get a photo of him. He was Special Forces, so maybe you can get it from his army record, or maybe Google has pictures of him at his senior prom. But it would be good to know him if we see him."

"On it."

"Laurie, you should call Cindy Spodek and see if the Bureau has anything on Churasick that they can share with us." Cindy is a friend of Laurie's and mine who is second in command in the FBI's Boston office. We've helped each other out on a number of occasions.

I turn to Eddie Dowd. "Eddie, we want to make sure we get all information on the poisoning investigation turned over to us in discovery. Dylan will argue it has nothing to do with the Oliva and Minardo murders, but that's bullshit. Threaten to go to Judge Koenig and Dylan will cave.

"And just a general note for everyone to think about. We haven't been able to identify who would have wanted Oliva dead, and why. I understand that he's a politician, and there are people who can prosper from him being out of the picture. But that's true of all politicians, and not many of them wind up getting dug up by Tara in Eastside Park.

"Okay, everyone, let's go back to work. And happy New Year."

New Year's Day is right up there with Thanksgiving and Christmas.

It doesn't necessarily have the great meal going for it, though that can be arranged. But it definitely has great college football bowl games. It used to be even better, before there was a playoff system and those games were usually played on a different day.

I also view New Year's Day as Christmas hump day. Laurie's Christmas lasts four months, and it's half over when the New Year comes around. It's not the home stretch, but at least it's progress.

So all in all, it's pretty damn good.

We woke up this morning to about six inches of snow, much to the delight of Tara and Hunter. Sebastian is less enthused about it, probably since walking in the stuff involves extra effort. He would like it if Tara and Hunter would pull him around in a wagon.

I take them for their morning walk, though I avoid Eastside Park. The last time we walked in the park in the snow it didn't go so well; I'm afraid this time Tara would dig up a governor or senator.

As we get back, I hear the phone ringing. Laurie gets it and hands it to me. "It's Sam."

"He's back, and he's got friends," Sam says when I get on.

"What are you talking about?"

"Drew Churasick. He flew into town from Detroit three days ago."

"Under that name?"

"No, he used the same fake name as before, Ronald Devers. He rented a car under that name again."

"But you're still sure his real name is Churasick?"

"I'm pretty sure it is. It's definitely not Devers; Devers doesn't exist."

"Do you know where he is now?"

"Not yet. Leon is trying to trace his credit card usage, but he might have used a different card than last time. If we can't trace it that way, we'll go through all the local hotels individually to see if he registered under Devers."

"What did you mean when you said, 'He's got friends'?"

"He flew in with three other people, all men. The tickets were purchased at the same time, and they sat together. I have their names, but I think they're all fake. We're checking that out now."

"And you know that they haven't left town?"

"They haven't flown out under those names, that's for sure. And the rental car has not been returned. So it's a good bet they are still in the area. But we're going to try and locate them."

"Let me know, Sam. This is important."

Laurie has been listening in on my side of the conversation, so when I get off, I tell her the full context.

She shares my view of how important this is. "Just using

a fraudulent identification for airplane travel is a felony by itself, Andy. These people wouldn't be doing it for a pleasure trip."

"I know."

"And suddenly whatever is going on requires four of them."

"It's possible there were four last time also," I say. "We wouldn't have known that; we were just going by the phone behind Theresa's house and the rental car."

"If our suspicions are correct, that Churasick was definitely involved in the Minardo death and probably responsible for Bobby's poisoning, then their presence here has to be seen as ominous." Laurie makes the word *ominous* sound really ominous.

"Do you have Bobby well protected in the hospital?"

She nods. "Yes. Corey's made arrangements that he feels will definitely prevent this from happening again. And the cops have been put on notice at Pete's level, so they will be vigilant too."

"Good."

"You could be a target."

"That wouldn't make sense."

"Let me get a pen so I can remember what to put on the tombstone . . . 'His death didn't make sense.'"

"Without me the investigation would be carried on by Bobby's defense team, whoever they are. And by you and Corey and Marcus. It would also draw the police in closer."

"Your reputation is such that you might be seen as a particular threat."

"Okay, I'll be careful."

"You need to stay alive. You don't want to miss the NFL playoffs and Super Bowl."

I hadn't thought of that. "You're right; that is something to live for."

The new discovery material contains an expected but unwelcome development.

Dylan has subpoenaed Bobby's cell phone records and learned what Sam has already told us, that Bobby's phone was at Oliva's house around the time of the murder, and in the park soon after. Dylan also knows that Bobby still had his phone after the crash and in the hospital, so there is no arguing that it was lost or stolen.

On one level it doesn't change much. Oliva's blood in Bobby's car obviously means they were together, phone or no phone. And since I've obviously known all of this for a while, I've come up with a theory of the case that covers it.

Bobby was unconscious in the car after the crash and had a level of drugs in his system that could have been lethal. There is absolutely no reason that the killer, Bobby, and Oliva could not have been in the car together. If Bobby was unconscious, probably from administered drugs, he would have no recollection of it and would have had no ability to resist.

The story makes sense to me and covers all the bases, but it is hard to imagine a jury buying it.

I haven't been to Charlie's Sports Bar in a while, which for me is unusual. Back in the pre-Laurie days, I used to go every night. Vince and Pete Stanton were always there at our regular table, and we'd drink beer, eat burgers and fries, watch sports, and insult one another. That's not all we did. Vince would also belch a lot and we'd scream at the televisions, as if that could influence the results.

But I'm going there tonight, not because I'm still paying the tab for all three of us, which I am, but mostly because I want to talk to Pete Stanton about the case. He is technically in the opposition camp, but I trust him, and he's the only cop I know who doesn't despise me. Pete only claims to.

When I get here, I see that Pete is sitting by himself at our table. That can only mean one thing: Vince must be in the bathroom. But as I get closer, I see that there are no plates or glasses in Vince's spot. If Vince is not here on a night when there is a college football playoff game, then he is not in the bathroom . . . he is in the hospital. Or dead.

"Well, look who's here," Pete says.

"Where's Vince?"

"Where's Vince? He's home. He was supposed to be here . . . hell, he lives here . . . but he just called and said he couldn't make it."

"Why?"

"Why? I'll tell you why. Because he couldn't get a dog sitter. You believe that? A dog sitter. Vince Sanders is not drinking beer and watching a playoff game because he couldn't get a dog sitter. This is all your fault."

"My fault? How do you figure that?"

"First of all, you wouldn't take the damn dog. You take dogs from everywhere, but suddenly you draw the line at Vince. And then you're such a dog nut, you took over his mind. It's like a cult; he's not drinking beer, he's drinking Kool-Aid."

"So he likes Duchess?"

Pete laughs derisively. "Yeah, I'd say so. The other night I'm trying to watch the LSU game and he's showing me pictures of her in bed. And I'm not talking about a dog bed; I'm talking about Vince's bed."

I laugh myself. "I don't believe it."

"Believe it. He thinks she's a genius because she took a dog biscuit. Don't all dogs eat biscuits? Does it have to be the Albert Einstein of dogs to eat a damn biscuit?"

"I'm sorry, Pete. Really I am."

"No, you're not. You wanted Vince to cross over to the dark side, and you pulled it off. Pretty soon he'll be going door-to-door with pamphlets, trying to recruit people. Well, you two are not getting me."

"Fair enough. Won't even try."

The waitress brings me a beer and follows it with a burger and crisp french fries. I've been here often enough that formal ordering became unnecessary long ago.

I think it's best I give Pete a little time to cool off, so we just eat quietly and watch the game. At halftime, I bring up the case.

"You heard what happened at the hospital?"

"Yeah. I heard."

"Any progress on finding out who did it?"

"I don't know. I'm in homicide; if your boy died, it would be my case."

"So you haven't heard anything?"

"Far as I know there are no suspects."

"Then let me help you out. The same guy that did it killed Theresa Minardo and probably Alex Oliva."

"Come on, I'd rather hear about Vince's dog than your defense attorney garbage."

"Which reminds me, did you know there's a band named Garbage?"

"Of course. They're great."

"Ricky says the same thing. But I'm serious, Pete. There's a guy out there who you should be looking for."

"You got a name?"

"I do, and I even have his picture."

Pete looks surprised; that's the last thing he expected me to say. I take out a copy of the photograph that Sam found for me and put it on the table. "His name is Drew Churasick; he lives in Detroit."

"Why should I be looking for him?" Pete has learned over time that when I say things like this, it is at least worth the effort to take it seriously.

I want to be protective of our case, so I don't want to give up too much information. "I can't say right now, Pete. But I am not making this up. I'm in the process of learning more about Churasick's background, and I'll share with you what I can. But he's someone for you to at least have on your radar. And you should know he has at least three friends with him."

"What do you think he's done?"

"I told you . . . he murdered Alex Oliva and Theresa Minardo."

Pete frowns. "Which means your client didn't."

"Exactly."

"Color me skeptical." But he folds the photo and puts it in his pocket. Then, "Let's watch the game. Unless you have to rush home to tuck your dogs into bed, too?"

Vince apparently stopped giving Duchess biscuits long enough to set up a meeting for me with Aaron Widener.

Widener is now the early favorite to become New Jersey's next governor now that Alex Oliva has departed. We're meeting at Widener's campaign office in Elizabeth, located in the district he represents as a state senator.

The main floor, which I walk through on the way to Widener's office, is busy with people working. The high energy has an intangible feeling of optimism to it. These people seem to think they are riding a winner, and all indications are that they are correct.

Once I'm in Widener's office and sitting across from him, he asks, "You got something on Vince?"

"What do you mean?"

"He just about begged me to see you. Vince generally is the one who likes to be begged. It was an unusual look for him, so I figured maybe you had a picture of him naked with a goat, or something."

"That's an image I'm going to have a tough time getting out of my mind."

Widener laughs. "Sorry about that. I'm glad to have

Vince owe me one; maybe he'll stop running editorials against me. What can I do for you?"

"Richard Minchner is a large contributor of yours." It is as if I just wiped the smile off Widener's face with a smile-removing rag. I hadn't even known if it was true that Minchner gave to him, but based on his reaction it obviously is.

"So?" he challenges.

"Why do you think that is?"

Widener's voice has gotten markedly colder. "Because he likes my policies. I'm pro-business, and he's a successful businessman."

"So were you surprised when you read the story about him and Alex Oliva?"

"No, because I knew it was a load of crap that your client was peddling. I even called Vince at the time and told him so. He didn't believe me, but I'll bet he wishes he had."

"What made you so sure?"

"Minchner might have given money to Alex. He gives money to a lot of people; it's his way of covering his bases. Can't blame him for that. But that much? There was no chance."

"So it didn't worry you? Oliva was your big competition."

Now Widener is noticeably angry. "And now he's not. Somebody else will come along; politics has a tendency to fill vacuums. If it was Alex or someone else, I'm not afraid of a challenge."

"Not with people like Richard Minchner behind you."

"Look, Carpenter. I heard about you, but I don't like your tone. And I am telling you right now that it is not a good idea to mess with the wrong people."

"Is that a threat?"

"This meeting is over, and you can tell Vince I'm pissed at him for setting it up."

I smile. "Great talking to you."

I get up and leave. I hope the first thing he does when I'm out the door is call Minchner and tell him what I said.

Meeting with Widener has been just another fun stop on the Andy Carpenter friendship tour. But it was interesting, and not just because Widener had a lot to gain from Oliva's death. As motives go, winning the governorship of New Jersey is a fairly substantial one.

More interesting to me is the reaction he had to my questions about Minchner. The only reason Widener would react so negatively is if he had something to hide. Of course, that something might not be complicity in a murder of his rival. It could be sensitivity to Minchner's status as a major political supporter, and the possibility that I could be searching for something illegal or unethical in their arrangement.

It's a piece of information to have and file; hopefully at some point it will make more sense than it does now. And hopefully Bobby won't be languishing in prison by the time it all comes together.

I am now full-on believing in Bobby's innocence. That is a relief; I would not relish enabling a murderer to go free. But it increases the pressure exponentially; I sure as hell do not want an innocent man to spend his life in prison.

Not on my watch.

Laurie and Corey Douglas are waiting for me when I get home. Simon Garfunkel is here as well, playing with Tara and Hunter.

Of all the team members, Simon clearly has the best job.

We go into the kitchen and Laurie pours everyone coffee. "We have some news to update you on," she says.

"I hope it's good. I'm not in the mood for bad."

"I would describe it as a mixed bag. Corey, why don't you go first?"

"Okay. I started tailing Richard Minchner as you asked. As discussed, I wasn't trying to find out anything or really learn where he was going. I just wanted him to know he was being watched. Actually, doing that bad a job of tailing somebody, even on purpose, is professionally embarrassing."

"But mission accomplished?" I ask.

"Oh, definitely. He sent a flunky, a guy named James Pritchett, to warn me off."

"I've met Pritchett; he's Minchner's right-hand man. I'm sure he scared the hell out of you."

"We had a delightful conversation. He told me to stop following Minchner, and I told him to kiss my ass."

"Is that all that was said?"

Corey shakes his head. "No, he said Minchner was not to be messed with, and I said neither was Andy Carpenter. I figured it couldn't hurt to exaggerate a bit."

"Good. Now you can just show yourself occasionally; when he doesn't see you, he'll assume you're there but doing a better job of concealing yourself. What else have you got for me?"

Laurie takes over. "Two things. The first is a beauty: Theresa Minardo was having an affair with Richard Minchner. It had been going on for almost two years."

"I'm not surprised, but how do you know that?"

"I interviewed one of her coworkers, Katie Corneau."

"Really? I talked with her early on, and she didn't say anything about that."

Laurie smiles. "Have you ever noticed that women aren't inclined to open up to you?"

I nod. "Now that you mention it, I have noticed that. It started in preschool."

"Well, it's ongoing. Katie did not like Minchner or how he treated Theresa. Katie would never break her confidence in life, but now that Theresa has been murdered, she thought that someone should know about it. That someone turned out to be me."

"So Theresa went to meet Minchner at the Hilton that night, he sent a damn car for her, and while she was gone, the explosive device was placed in her garage without her there to notice."

Laurie nods. "I would say that seems to be a reasonable hypothesis."

"You said there were two things? And we haven't gotten to the bad part yet."

"I spoke to Cindy Spodek. She was not familiar with Churasick, but she asked around and did not like what she heard."

"Which was?"

"Churasick was Special Forces, deployed to Iraq twice. He was dishonorably discharged, but the reason is under seal. There are rumors that civilian deaths were involved. The army would want to underplay that, but get rid of Churasick at the same time, and they apparently accomplished both."

"What's he doing now?"

"Unclear. After the army he started doing security work, including for one of Minchner's companies. Ironically he went back to Iraq for a while in that civilian capacity. Then he seemed to drop out of sight. Here comes one of the bad parts: he is considered extremely dangerous and doesn't seem to possess a conscience."

"And the other bad part?"

"He is thought to be connected to Jerry Conti, though that is not confirmed."

"The name is familiar but I can't place it."

"That's because you've lived a sheltered life. Conti is organized crime, originally out of Detroit, but according to Cindy, as crime families in other cities have aged and weakened, he's expanded his operation and moved in elsewhere. He sucks up business wherever he goes. Think of him as the Amazon.com of scumbags."

"And now he's moving into New Jersey?"

"Cindy's people didn't know that, but she said she wouldn't put it past him. He does have a foothold in Philadelphia; he can cover South Jersey from there."

"Wouldn't Junior have something to say about his moving in here?" Joseph Russo, Jr., has controlled northern New Jersey, from a criminal standpoint, ever since his father took a bullet in his head.

"Russo's operation is not anywhere close to what it was. Cindy's people think that he'd be willing to make a deal to coexist with Conti; it could even work in his favor, especially if Conti sweetened the deal to get Russo to go along. He could even wind up with more money and manpower in the process."

"How sure is Cindy about all this?"

"She says that they are not at all sure, but I don't think she'd be telling me unless it was very likely."

I call Sam to find out if he has located Churasick yet, but Sam says that he has not. The phone Churasick used the night Theresa Minardo died is not sending out a GPS signal; Sam thinks Churasick trashed it and is using a new one.

When I get off, I say to Laurie and Corey, "I'd say we're making progress; at least we've identified the enemy."

The reputation of Mayor Alex Oliva is not exactly thriving since he went to that great City Hall in the sky.

Acting Mayor Oscar Womack, if previously not an ally of Oliva's then at least not an adversary, has started to publicly make noises about the state of the city government as he has found it.

He has already replaced the planning commissioner, Jason Civale, who was arrested on the drug-possession charge just days after Oliva's death. But Womack is starting to talk about uncovering other corruption, though without specifically blaming Oliva.

He is tiptoeing around his criticism of the police commissioner, Randy Bauer. Womack is clearly upset that the police under Bauer have made no progress in identifying the perpetrators of the bombing at the bus station. And Bauer was an Alex Oliva hire, which automatically puts him on Womack's radar.

However, Bauer is also Womack's major opposition for the November mayoralty election, so any criticism of Bauer by Womack might seem overtly political.

Womack is also careful not to be too obvious in his negative view of Oliva's overall administration. So he tries to be subtle, and it comes off, at least to me, as sounding like he doesn't want to publicly talk ill about the dead while between the lines talking ill about the dead.

I don't have a hell of a lot of interest in Paterson government, but I am interested in Alex Oliva. If in fact there was corruption, then it is at least remotely possible that Oliva was involved with some unsavory, if not criminal, elements. There is always the chance that a falling out resulted in those "elements" forcibly removing him from office.

More important, those powerful enemies would not want him to have the power of the governorship, where he could do them a hell of a lot more damage than as mayor of Paterson.

That theory has so many suppositions and guesses as to make it beyond unreliable, but unfortunately it's all I have at the moment.

Since Acting Mayor Womack is in a far better position than I am to know what is going on, I place a call to him, hoping to meet again. It's a long shot; he's got a lot on his plate and he'll probably take the view that one meeting is plenty. Most people find one meeting with me to be more than plenty.

I leave word with one of his assistants and am surprised when I get a call back from the same person a half hour later. Womack would have time for me in a half hour, if I can get there in time. So I'm out the door and on the way.

Sure enough, thirty minutes later I'm led into Womack's office. He looks a lot more harried than he did last time; his jacket is off and his tie is loosened. But he manages to have a smile on his face.

"Thanks for seeing me. I'm sure you're busy."

"No problem. Compared to the rest of my day, this is a vacation. Besides, I want you to vote for me in November."

"I'm considering my options. So being mayor of Paterson doesn't have the glamour everybody thinks it does?"

He smiles. "Not so much." Then, "To what do I owe this visit?"

"I'd like to know what you've learned about Alex Oliva since you've been in this job."

He looks wary. "That's a pretty open-ended question."

"I save my yes-or-no questions for cross-examinations."

He starts to answer, then hesitates for at least twenty long seconds. "Are we off the record?"

"Well, I'm not in the media, so I have no place to report it. And I can't repeat what you say in court because that would be hearsay. So I think you're safe."

"Well, let's just say I'm surprised by what I've found. I thought Alex was looking for dirt, and he was, but he wasn't cleaning it up. The opposite was true, and every time I turn over a rock, I don't like what I find under it."

"This extends beyond Civale, the planning commissioner?"

"The drug thing? Yeah, but that's nothing. I don't blame Alex for that; he vetted Civale and nothing turned up."

"So who else?"

"I really can't say at this point, but change is coming. I've made no secret of that. By the time of the election, people will be able to see my team for who they are. Then they'll like what I've done or not."

"Has Richard Minchner's name been coming up in all this?"

Womack looks surprised. "You're still focused on him?

No, I haven't heard his name since you were here last time."

"He was having an affair with Theresa Minardo."

"Is that right?" Womack shows even more surprise. "Well, what do you know? What's the expression? Politics makes strange bedfellows? In this case that's literally true."

"Yes, it is."

"Then that makes Bobby Nash's original story even less likely. Why would Theresa come to him with evidence that implicates her boyfriend and her boss in an illegal contribution?"

It's a good point, and one I have already thought of. "That's just one of the questions I can't answer." Then I change the subject. "Any progress on the bombing investigation?"

Womack frowns. "Since we're still talking in confidence, our police commissioner couldn't catch a cold. He doesn't know who did it or why they did. Both of those are significant questions to answer, don't you think?"

I nod. "And he wants to be the next mayor instead of you."

"Then he could bring that same level of expertise and execution to the whole city. What a disaster."

"What do you think of Aaron Widener?"

"I think he's going to be our next governor, so I'm going to have to work with him."

"I spoke with him. He got upset when I mentioned Minchner."

"I really have nothing to say about that. Hopefully good reporters will find out what is going on there, if anything."

"Bobby Nash was a good reporter."

"The operative word there is *was*. Sounds like you're not getting anywhere?"

"Making progress, but never rapid enough. The trial is bearing down on us."

"I wish you well, unless Bobby is guilty. Whatever Alex and Theresa might have done, they didn't deserve the death penalty."

"While you've been looking into Alex's time in office, has the name Jerry Conti come up?"

Womack thinks for a few seconds, searching his memory bank. "Sounds familiar, but I don't think I've heard it lately, and I can't place it. Who is he?"

"He is, as they say, a person of interest."

Vince has information about Richard Minchner to discuss with me, so I suggest we meet at Charlie's.

"Can't make it tonight. Too much going on."

"No dog sitter?"

Vince hesitates, probably surprised that I knew his problem. "You been talking to Pete?" Then, "I don't like leaving her alone; she's very sensitive. Is there anything wrong with that?" he asks, in a challenging tone.

I laugh. "Not a thing, Vince. Not a thing. Believe me, I get it."

"So can you come over here?"

"Sure. Laurie will be out at Edna's bridal shower, but Ricky has a sleepover, and our dogs don't need a sitter."

"Edna's bridal shower? I would rather attend a mass root canal."

I feed the dogs their dinner, take them for a quick walk, and head for Vince's house. He lives in Leonia, which is about ten minutes west of the George Washington Bridge.

Even though it's dark when I get there and maybe thirty degrees outside, Vince is in his front yard playing with Duchess, who is absolutely adorable.

"Watch this." Vince picks up a tennis ball and throws it about five feet away. "Go get it, girl. Go get it."

Duchess just sits at Vince's feet; she has no interest in going to get it. Vince walks over, picks up the ball, and throws it again, this time an even shorter distance. "Come on, Duchess. Fetch it, girl."

No movement at all from Duchess; if anything, she seems amused by Vince's efforts.

"Smart as a whip," I say.

"She just doesn't want to show off. She's been getting the ball every time until you showed up."

I nod. "She seems like the humble sort. Can we go inside? It's cold out here."

We go inside, and after Vince gives Duchess a biscuit, we sit down to talk. "So I've found out all I can about Minchner. I've called in every favor I could."

"I'm listening."

"You can also be reading." Vince hands me a folder. "All the detail is in here, everything that everybody said. Take it home with you; I have copies."

I flip through the folder, impressed by the effort Vince put into this; he hasn't been spending all his time playing fetch. "Bottom-line it for me. What do people think about him?"

"Well, first of all, no one thinks Minchner's the brightest bulb in the chandelier, that's for sure."

"That's the impression I had as well. But he runs a huge business."

"Maybe. Maybe not. Here's the situation. He grew the business not by building from the ground up, but by purchasing other businesses. Where he got the funding to do so is a question that no one seems to know the answer to, but everyone has suspicions about.

"The other surprising thing is that every business he bought experienced a sudden growth spurt after he took over. So there's either something going on, or he's the luckiest dumb man in history."

"Has the name Jerry Conti come up?"

Vince looks surprised. "Jerry Conti?"

"You know who he is?"

"Of course I know who he is. But nobody has mentioned him in connection with Minchner. That doesn't mean it's not possible; it actually would explain a lot. But if Conti is pulling the strings, he's doing it in the dark."

Vince doesn't have much more to tell me, though I want to read what's in the folder when I get home. I would go home right away, but Vince has to spend a half hour showing me all the other tricks that Duchess has no interest in doing.

Vince keeps giving her treats and praise anyway; Duchess is definitely in charge of this relationship. By the next time I come over, she'll be having him fetch stuff.

But Vince has come through with good information on Minchner, who is the guy I am increasingly focusing on. He's becoming, possibly along with Jerry Conti, the person I am hoping to sell to the jury as a credible killer.

At this point it's a tough sell.

Eddie Dowd left a message on my cell that we've received discovery on the hospital poisoning, and that he is having it sent to my house.

He says there's not much to speak of, that the cops are basically nowhere on it. I'll read it when I get home, especially if Laurie is not back yet from Edna's bridal shower.

As I pull up, I see that Laurie doesn't seem to be home yet. She likes to park on the street, and I don't see her car. I drive into our driveway and open the garage with the automatic opener. I have to admit that ever since Theresa Minardo died in that explosion, I get a little nervous each time I press that button.

But I manage to get into the garage without blowing up, so I feel confident enough to close it automatically as well. I am Andy Carpenter, the death-defying attorney.

I leave the garage through the side door and walk toward the house. My plan is to take the dogs for a walk and then read through Vince's folder and the new discovery documents.

"Welcome home, asshole."

Two men, two large men, are standing on the lawn between me and the door. I can see them in the fairly dim light coming through the windows of the house. Their voices start our dogs barking inside.

The size of the men doesn't matter because the guy on the left is holding a gun in his hand. It's in his left hand, which I for some reason notice, even though that fact is of absolutely no consequence. I assume he is holding it in a hand capable of aiming and pulling the trigger. At this range he could be holding it by his toes and not miss.

I am petrified; my legs are literally shaking. If anything, that fear increases when his next statement is "We're going for a little drive in your car. Unless you'd rather die here."

I haven't said a word; I don't think I could even if I wanted to. Lefty makes a motion with his gun, meaning I should start walking back toward the garage. In case I didn't get the message, he says, "Let's go, lawyer. Now."

My mind kicks into gear; I'm thinking if I can make a sudden dash for the side of the garage, I might take them by surprise and make it into my neighbor's backyard. I know my way around back there and they wouldn't, so in the dark I might be able to get away. They might also be reluctant to fire a gun in this quiet neighborhood.

It's a pathetic plan, but once I get into the car with these guys, I am dead meat. I cannot let that happen.

I'm about five feet from the garage door. I think the two guys are another seven feet or so behind me, but my back is to them so I can't be sure. I'm about to make a break for it when I hear one of them say something that sounds like "Hey."

I think they're talking to me, but then I hear some kind of rustling noise, so I stop and turn. Even though it's obviously still dark, my eyes have adjusted some and I see Lefty's gun go flying about ten feet off to the side, near the driveway.

Lefty himself moves in a different direction from the gun. He goes backward as I see Marcus Clark hit him with the club that is attached to Marcus's shoulder. Lefty lands in a heap and doesn't move.

The other guy has taken a moment to react, but finally and stupidly moves aggressively toward Marcus. It doesn't work out well for him.

Marcus grabs him and throws him against the garage wall, as he might a sack of flour, or in this case a sack of shit. The guy hits the wall face-first. I hear a crunch and an agonized moan; they sound simultaneous, but the crunch must come first because that's obviously what causes the moan.

"Marcus," I say, because what else is there to say?

He doesn't answer, just picks up by the collar the guy that he threw against the wall and starts dragging him to where Lefty is lying on the ground.

Except Lefty is not there anymore. I look, and in a moment of horror I see that he has regrouped and made it over toward the driveway, where his gun is. He gets to the gun before I can reach it, possibly because I am frozen in place and unable to move.

Lefty picks up the gun and points it at Marcus, and the sound of the gunshot is deafening in the driveway.

Marcus just stands there, and for a moment I think that he is truly Superman, and that the bullet has bounced off him. Or maybe he's caught it in his teeth.

But then I see that Lefty is once again lying on the

ground, silent and unmoving, and I realize that he is the one that has been shot. Laurie is standing in the driveway, holding her gun in her hand, so it's a pretty good bet that she shot him.

Laurie is great looking 24-7, but she has never looked any better than this.

"Are you okay?" she asks.

I nod my head, while trying unsuccessfully to get my legs to stop shaking. "I'm fine. Just another day in the lawyer business." Then, "How was the bridal shower?"

"Well, fortunately it ended early."

Because it's hard for me to dial with my hand shaking, Laurie calls Pete and then 911 to report what has happened.

Laurie has confirmed that Lefty is dead; she nailed him in the chest with one shot in the dark, desperately trying to do so in a split second before he could shoot Marcus. It was a remarkable feat.

That's my girl.

The guy that Marcus rammed into the garage wall has come to, and Laurie has placed him in handcuffs. That she had handcuffs in the house all this time but never shared that information with me is interesting in itself, but a subject for another time.

Some neighbors are cautiously gathering at the end of our driveway, having heard the shot. I call out to them that there's nothing to see here, a statement that is rendered ridiculous when three police cars, lights flashing, pull up.

Corey also arrives; I guess Laurie must have called him as well. Between him and Laurie they know a few of the cops, which enables those cops to tell the good guys from the bad guys.

An ambulance shows up, and they provide treatment of some sort for the garage-wall guy. They have no trouble determining that treatment on Lefty is not called for, and I'm sure the coroner's van will be here soon.

It's a big day in the neighborhood.

Pete arrives with two of his homicide detectives, though no homicide has been committed. He's all-business, asking a series of questions that get me to describe exactly what happened, with Laurie and Marcus standing there to correct me if I miss anything.

When I'm finished, Pete asks, "So Laurie shot that one and Marcus took care of that one, while you just stood there pissing in your pants?"

I nod. "That pretty much sums it up, yes."

"Do you know who they are?"

"You'd have to compare their IDs, which I assume are fake, with their travel records flying in from Detroit, but—"

"How do you know they flew in from Detroit?"

I'm not about to tell him that; it would mean throwing Sam under the bus. "I investigated; you should try it sometime." Then, "As I was about to say, I believe very strongly they are two of the three associates of Drew Churasick, who I warned you about."

Pete turns to Laurie. "You agree with everything this pain in the ass just said?"

She nods. "I do."

Pete then turns back to me. "What were these two guys doing here?"

"Planning to kill me."

"Why would they do that, other than the fact that you're annoying and obnoxious?"

"Because they think I am making progress toward finding the real killer of Oliva and Theresa Minardo. And their ultimate boss doesn't want that to happen."

"Who's their ultimate boss?"

"Jerry Conti."

I can see Pete react in surprise; obviously he knows who Conti is. "These guys work for Jerry Conti?"

"Technically they probably work for Churasick, who then works for Conti. We think Conti is trying to move in here. He's probably picked this area because the homicide cops are incompetent."

"Boys, boys . . . ," Laurie says.

"Where's Ricky?" Pete asks, which ranks as his first considerate question.

"A sleepover at a friend's house."

"Good."

It's another two hours before we've given our statements and the various forensics, medical, and coroner's people have cleared out. Corey and Marcus leave as well, and finally it's just me and Laurie.

She pours us a couple of glasses of wine, and we sit down on the couch in the living room; neither of us would be able to sleep right now if we tried.

"You had Marcus watching me."

She nods. "Correct."

"You didn't tell me you were doing it."

Another nod. "Also correct."

"You didn't think I could protect myself."

Still another nod. "Three *correct*s in a row; you're on a roll."

"I had a plan, you know. I was going to get away from them."

"You had a plan and they had a gun. Here's a tip, Andy: never bring a plan to a gunfight."

"They would have killed me; you saved my life."

"It was a selfish act. I would dread getting back to the dating scene."

"You also saved Marcus's life."

She shakes her head. "No, he would have figured something out. That's the difference. You're you, and he's Marcus."

If we're right that Jerry Conti is behind much of this, as part of his plan to move into the Paterson area, the key question is why.

Paterson and Passaic County are not particularly strong economic areas; there have to be more lucrative places for Conti to place his focus. But he seems to have chosen to come here, and I assume that choice is based on logic and potential profit.

He may or may not be Minchner's silent business partner and financial benefactor, but it's worth investigating, and doing so quickly. We are running out of time.

I call Sam and ask him to do a phone check on Minchner, to see if he has had any contact with Conti. Sam can probably get Conti's number; Sam can get everything. But at the least he can discover if Minchner called any phone located in the Detroit area, which is Conti's home base.

The other puzzling thing is why Oliva was killed in the first place. Assuming Minchner and perhaps Conti were behind it, the question, as always, is why? It's hard to understand what Oliva, in his position as mayor, could have done to make his death necessary.

Theresa Minardo's murder, in my mind, has always been about pinning blame on Bobby Nash. He had reason to hold a grudge against Oliva and Theresa, so he would have had an obvious motive for the prosecution to grab on to.

But maybe she was a more important player in some way I don't understand. Her affair with Minchner increases that possibility, but I still have no idea why he would have wanted her dead, or why she would have turned on Oliva by providing Bobby with the fake checks.

Maybe I can tell the jury to wait a few months while I figure things out.

There is a bit of good news. Bobby has mostly recovered from the poisoning. He's not all the way back, which in a way is good because it will keep him in the hospital, and not jail.

But the attack on his life should enable us to put enough pressure on Judge Koenig to keep him there for a while, and to provide him with extra protection when he does go to the jail. Now that they have gone after both Bobby and me, the cops are taking it seriously. Pete Stanton, to his credit, has seen to that.

I'm at the hospital to visit Bobby for the first time in a while, and the first thing he says to me is "I heard what happened to you. I'm sorry that getting involved with me caused that to happen."

"Who told you?"

"Vince."

"Vince has a big mouth."

"That's not exactly breaking news." Then, "Are they going to let me stay here during the trial?"

"I hope so; at least for part of it. If they do, you'll be brought to the courtroom and then back here each day.

If you don't feel up to it, I'm sure the court will let you attend through Zoom."

"No, I want to be there."

"We'll work it out, but either way you'll be well protected. They're worried you'll get killed while in their custody; that's a bad look for the authorities."

"Do we know who tried to kill me. And you?"

"We have suspicions, but nothing we can prove. Did you ever hear the name Jerry Conti?"

"No. Who is he?"

"An unpleasant enemy for us to have. And what would you say if I told you that Richard Minchner and Theresa Minardo were having an affair for two years?"

"Are you serious?"

"I am."

"Then why would she have tried to sandbag him with those forged checks?"

"Maybe she wasn't. Maybe it was all planned with him, and they both knew that he could prove it wasn't real. Maybe the whole thing was planned in advance to end the way it did."

"Why would they do that?"

"That, my boy, is one of the very key questions."

I leave the hospital, and when I'm out the door, I turn my cell phone on. There are signs all over the hospital prohibiting cell phone use, for some unexplained reason, yet I see people using them all the time.

I don't know why, but I feel compelled to follow rules like that. In this case, I imagine that if I don't, some poor patient will be lying in his bed, screaming in agony, *"There's a cell phone on! Turn it off . . . please . . . turn it off!"*

When I turn it back on, there's a message from Laurie to call her. When I do, she says, "You got a rather unusual call."

"From who?"

"Nancy Oliva, Alex's wife, now his widow. She wants to see you."

Alex Oliva lived with his wife, Nancy, at Thirty-ninth and Park, which is not far from my house on Forty-second, near Nineteenth Avenue.

According to the prosecution, Alex died here at the hands of Bobby Nash, before being taken to Eastside Park and dumped there.

I have no idea why Nancy Oliva wants to see me; I hope it's not to berate me for defending her husband's killer. I doubt that's it, since she would have had plenty of time to do that already.

I'm encouraged when she greets me at the door with a smile on her face, albeit a sad one. She invites me in, and the first thing I notice are packed boxes everywhere, though the furniture is still in place.

"Are you moving?"

She nods. "Yes. Going back home to Seattle. I met Alex at the University of Washington, and I haven't lived there since. Paterson has been home ever since, but it has suddenly lost its appeal for me."

"I understand."

"Alex loved this city."

"I do as well," I say, because I do.

She offers me coffee and I accept, so we sit in the kitchen. "I debated whether to call you."

"I'm certainly curious why you did."

"I've been thinking about what happened that horrible day. I certainly don't know for sure, but I think the police may have arrested the wrong man."

I am both surprised and pleased to hear this. "Why do you say that?"

"There are a few reasons. I may be wrong in each case, but taken together they have given me pause. I received two phone calls, here at the house, one the day before Alex died, and one that day. In each case the caller identified himself as Bobby Nash and demanded to meet with Alex; he made vague threats if Alex did not agree."

I just nod and wait; I've known this from the discovery.

"Looking back, there were a couple of things about the calls that bother me. First of all, why call him at home? He would have known Alex was in his office; why would he rather talk to me?"

I hope she's got something better than this, but I just have to wait to hear it.

"Then I realized that the number he called on . . . we had a number that was private, but fairly widely known. Members of the press called on it frequently. Alex enjoyed his encounters with reporters. But when the campaign started and the calls increased, we put in a private line just for a few close friends and colleagues, mostly high-level city officials, and we let the machine screen calls to the original line.

"The calls from Bobby Nash were on the new line; how would he have known that number? He could have had easy access to the other one.

"So these things were bothering me for a while, and yesterday I did something. I went online and watched an interview that Mr. Nash did on television around the time he wrote the story about Minchner and the campaign contribution. I was stunned by it."

"Why?" Now I was starting to get interested in what else she had to say.

"His voice; it was noticeably different. I used to be a speech therapist, a long time ago, but I still notice things like that. Actually, I can't help it; it's my training.

"But in this case, the timbre, the inflection, it was not the same. Mr. Carpenter, I don't think that was Bobby Nash on the phone." She still looks sad, but resolute.

"Would you testify to this?"

"I was hoping you wouldn't ask that, but I assumed you would, and if it's necessary, I would testify. Mr. Campbell expects me to testify for the prosecution, but I'm sure when I tell him what I've just told you, he will not want me to."

"Thank you." I wish she would not mention anything to Dylan, and then when he asks her the questions on the stand, she can sandbag him. But I have a feeling that's not her style.

I hesitate to ask my next question because I don't want to anger her. But I can't help myself. "Have you ever heard the name Jerry Conti?"

"No. I don't think so."

"What was Alex's relationship with Richard Minchner?"

"I really couldn't say; I think he was just a campaign contributor. But . . ." She hesitates, as if trying to decide whether to continue. "Mr. Minchner would have become less important to Alex because he had decided not to run for governor."

This is a bombshell. "Why?"

"I'm not sure. He was worried about something, but he hadn't shared it with me yet. All he told me was that he was needed in Paterson."

"Who else knew about this?" She must know the importance of this question.

"Very few people; I don't know exactly who. But Alex was going to announce it soon; he wanted to do it quickly so that his campaign staff could get other jobs. He was upset about the effect it would have on them."

"Would Richard Minchner have been one of the people Alex shared this news with?"

"I would strongly doubt it; I would say almost certainly not. It would have been limited to those people who needed to know; maybe some in city government. I just don't know who that is."

"So Aaron Widener would not have been informed?"

Her reaction is immediate. "Oh, no. Certainly not. One of the things that made Alex's decision a difficult one is that he knew that his dropping out would increase the chances that Widener would be governor. Alex was not fond of him at all. He also did not respect him; he referred to him as an empty suit."

I thank Nancy and leave, telling her that if I need her to testify, I'll give her plenty of notice. She again says she'd much rather not, and I respect that, but if I need her, I'll call her. And I will almost definitely need her.

One of the areas I didn't question her about was Oscar Womack's increasingly public view that he found questionable practices in Oliva's administration upon taking over as acting mayor. There was nothing to be gained from bringing it up; certainly she would support her husband.

A lot was going on with Alex Oliva, much of which I will probably never know. But by definition he was involved with dangerous people, and they killed him. Whether he was their enemy from the outset, or whether he was an ally that had outlived his usefulness, is a question I wish I could answer.

The news about Alex's intending not to run for governor might or might not be significant. That people like Minchner and Widener would probably not have known makes that significance less likely, but it's still interesting.

I wish I knew why Alex Oliva had made that momentous decision. It might be the key to everything.

Or maybe not.

Drew Churasick has dropped off the face of the earth, or at least off Sam's radar . . . which is basically the same thing.

He might well still be here in the area, using a different fake ID and different phone. Or he might have taken that fake ID and flown back to Detroit or gone somewhere else to do Jerry Conti's bidding.

We just don't know.

We also don't know where the third man who flew in with Churasick is. One of them was shot by Laurie, and another is in custody after Marcus used him to play handball with the side of the garage, but the third hasn't been heard from.

I do know that no additional attempts have been made on the lives of either Bobby or me. That is clearly a positive development, though obviously we don't know the reason for the hiatus, or when it might end.

One possibility could be that the killers have decided that attempting to eliminate us is not worth the attention it is getting, and that we might well lose at trial anyway.

They might also not terribly care whether we win or lose at trial. Police human nature is such that if the jury acquits Bobby, they will think the jury made the error, and that they arrested and charged the right person.

When O. J. Simpson was acquitted, the police did not instigate a new investigation hunting for the real killer. They, like most of America, thought that the jury blew it.

Since the mayor was the one murdered, the police might pay lip service to a new investigation, but their heart wouldn't likely be in it, and the killers might realize that. The key for them, therefore, was to get the police to believe Bobby did it, not necessarily to convict him.

With the trial getting ever closer, I've been spending more time with Eddie Dowd on our strategy, and reading the discovery more frequently and intensely.

At my direction, Eddie has prepared a change-of-venue motion to present to the court. He had Edna type it.

"When I called her, she asked me if I could think of something blue she could wear at her wedding," Eddie says.

"What did you tell her?"

"I told her to get a small ink stain on her dress, where no one could see it. I don't think she was thrilled with me."

"You just blew your chance to be a bridesmaid."

The change-of-venue motion covers in detail the press coverage of the killings and makes the obvious point that the proper place to have a trial of an accused mayor-killer is not in the city that had the victim as its mayor.

Judge Koenig will blow off the motion and deny it, which is fine. I'm not even that anxious to move the trial. But it will make a decent issue on which to base an appeal, if we wind up in that unfortunate position.

Eddie has also arranged for a couple of expert witnesses

to testify if we need them, though whether we use them will depend on what comes out of the prosecution's case.

I think we have an at least somewhat credible theory to present as our defense, but our success will likely hinge on offering up an alternate killer. We certainly have our suspicions, but unless Judge Koenig went to the Bozo the Clown School of Law, he will not allow suspicions to be introduced as evidence.

Enter Sam Willis to the rescue . . . sort of.

"Andy, I've got something pretty important," Sam says to me one afternoon on the phone. "Hilda picked it up."

"I'm listening."

"Two calls were placed today from Minchner's office to Jerry Conti."

"No way to know what they spoke about, I assume?"

"No. These aren't wiretaps, we're just checking phone records."

"I understand. Do you know how long they spoke?"

"Six minutes on the first call and eleven on the second. The calls were almost four hours apart."

"Sam, can you call Eddie Dowd and let him know the exact information about the calls? We might want to subpoena the phone records to use in court. Also give him the information for Churasick's phone's whereabouts the night of the murders."

"Will do."

"I've told him this already, but make sure he knows not to move forward with the subpoenas yet. I don't want Dylan to know we are after this information until the last minute."

"Got it."

While I know that Sam has got it, I'm going to call Eddie Dowd anyway to reiterate that he should hold off. At this point we can't afford mistakes . . . we're at trial time.

My name is Dylan Campbell. I am an attorney representing Passaic County and the State of New Jersey.

"I've been doing so for nine years. I'm sure you think that my role is an adversarial one, and to some degree you would be right. Mr. Carpenter will be representing the defendant, Robert Nash, and we will both be trying to win. Both of us will be trying very hard, believe me.

"But I, like all prosecutors everywhere, have a special obligation. More important than winning is finding the truth; we are in a search for it because only by getting to the truth and acting on it can justice be done.

"That is where you come in. Your job, and it is as important as anyone's job anywhere, is to decide what that truth is. You will hear competing versions, that's what trials are about, and you must cut through all of that and find your own truth . . . the real truth.

"The State of New Jersey has charged Robert Nash with the murders of Alex Oliva and Theresa Minardo. That is the truth as we see it. But we don't just bring our point of view to this courtroom; that's not how this works. We are obliged to bring evidence to back it up.

"I have been a part of many trials where the evidence

can be confusing, and complicated, and hard to wade through. This, I can say with certainty, is not one of those times.

"Don't be influenced by the packed gallery, or the press coverage that you may have read prior to today. Even though one of the victims had a very high public profile, this is no different than many other cases I have tried, and that juries like you have participated in.

"We will be able to place Mr. Nash at the scene of at least one of the crimes. There will also be substantial forensic evidence involving both crimes that you will find compelling and conclusive.

"You may not be aware of this, but in a criminal trial the prosecution, in this case me, does not have to demonstrate or prove motive. We only have to prove to you, beyond a reasonable doubt, that the defendant committed the crime. We do not have to tell you why or opine on what might have been going on inside his head.

"But even though we don't have to, in this case we will do exactly that. We will show you that Mr. Nash blamed the two victims, Mr. Oliva and Ms. Minardo, for destroying his career. The truth is that Mr. Nash destroyed his own career by running a bogus story maligning Mr. Oliva and a local, prominent businessman, Richard Minchner.

"But he took no personal blame or responsibility for what he had done. He made no secret of his hatred for Mr. Oliva and Ms. Minardo; you will see that very clearly. Finally that hatred boiled over into the most horrible violence, and two people lost their lives.

"Your decision, I would submit, will not be a difficult

one. But it will be a momentous one, because it will bring the justice that the State of New Jersey is intent on administering.

"Thank you for listening, and thank you very much for your service."

Judge Koenig asks me if I want to give my opening statement now or wait for the start of the defense case. As always, I want to do it now, to at least let the jury know there is another side to the story.

As I get up, I look around the courtroom. It is, as Dylan said, packed with spectators and media. Since the day that the Oliva murder was revealed, there has been intense interest in the case, no doubt because of his prominent position.

That is why I thought the change-of-venue motion should have succeeded, even though Judge Koenig denied it. I was pleased with his ruling, both because I was fine with the trial being here, and also because I think it presents an appeal opportunity, should we need one. But I think he ruled incorrectly.

Bobby Nash, over our objections and to my surprise, was moved to the jail yesterday. His health is now fine, and we have been promised that he will have extra security. It will mean solitary confinement in the short term, but that is better than the alternative.

He sits at the defense table in a suit and tie, between me and Eddie Dowd. As an ex-NFL linebacker, Eddie is borderline huge. Bobby is bigger than me but smaller than Eddie, so it looks like our defense team is on a tilt.

I don't stand at a podium like Dylan does. I like to walk around the room, making it feel more casual. Actually, it is more casual, as I don't script what I'm going to say. I basically know what points I want to cover, but I like the spontaneity that comes with not rehearsing.

"Ladies and gentlemen, when I give an opening statement, I do not usually refer to anything that the prosecutor has said. That's because what we lawyers say are just words, not evidence, as Judge Koenig will instruct you.

"So generally I just say what I have to say. I tell you the defense point of view, and then I'm happy to let the evidence speak for itself. But in this case I feel like I should respond to something Mr. Campbell told you.

"I'm paraphrasing here, and you may remember his exact words, but he basically said that while both sides want to win, the difference between us is that he and the State of New Jersey are unique in their determination to find the truth.

"He's right in that we both want to win, but if I have one wish in this trial, it is that the truth comes out. Because then both sides win, and Mr. Nash gets the freedom he deserves.

"And despite what Mr. Campbell told you, this case is quite complicated. It involves politics and power, with some sex thrown in, and nothing about those things is ever simple. There are players and motives behind the scenes, and you will have to think and analyze and understand the nuances. Your job is not an easy one, but you need to put in the effort, as I know you will.

"The police rushed to judgment in arresting Mr. Nash. Now, I admit that is something that defense attorneys often claim. The truth is, it is our go-to, knee-jerk defense. You could even say that we rush to make the judgment that it's a rush to judgment.

"But it has never been more true than in this case. And you will hear, from a very key witness, why that rushed judgment was based on incorrect information.

"So it was incorrect, but what it did was stop the investigation in its tracks. They decided that Mr. Nash was guilty and moved on. The net result is that he sits here, wrongly accused, while the real killer runs free.

"So I ask that you keep an open mind. The prosecution will be presenting evidence that they will claim makes it obvious Mr. Nash is guilty, an open-and-shut case. But I assure you that there are explanations for everything, so please understand that as we go along. We will provide those explanations when we present our case, and you will judge them against the prosecution's evidence. That is your job.

"I am certain that by the time we finish, you will be swimming in a sea of reasonable doubt. Not only that, but you will have a very good idea who the actual guilty party is, and you will know that it is not Mr. Nash.

"Thank you for listening."

Dylan surprises me with his first witness. It is Sidney Hoffman, Vince's boss and the publisher of the paper.

Despite the fact that the state does not have to prove motive, Dylan obviously thinks it is important enough to lead with it. I think it's a mistake on his part, but I understand why he is doing it. He is telling the jury a story and feels that it's best to start at the beginning.

Vince warned me that this might happen, and I knew that Hoffman's name was on the witness list, so I'm prepared. I know from Vince that Hoffman did not want to testify; he feels uncomfortable not supporting his people, even though Bobby is no longer one of those people.

Dylan takes him through his family history and how he came to be publisher of the paper. Basically, he climbed his way up the ladder by being his father's son, and his grandfather's grandson. The family ownership of the paper goes back way beyond that as well.

That's not to say he is unqualified. He was a journalism major at Northwestern and earned his Ph.D. He's a serious man and widely respected, even if nepotism was his entry ticket to the big dance.

"Mr. Hoffman, did your paper at any point publish a story by Mr. Nash concerning campaign contributions made by Richard Minchner to Mayor Oliva, in return for a construction contract?" Dylan asks.

"We did."

Dylan introduces a copy of the story into evidence and gets Hoffman to confirm that it is the story he meant.

"Did you approve the story before it ran?"

Hoffman nods. "I did."

"You were confident that it was correct?"

"Yes."

"Based on what?"

"Based on the assurance of our executive editor, Vince Sanders, that we had the documentation to back it up."

"You have confidence in Mr. Sanders?"

"I do, absolutely."

"Did the story turn out to be accurate?"

"It did not."

Dylan gets Hoffman to provide the details of how Oliva and Minchner both objected strenuously, filed lawsuits, and proved that the documents were faked.

Dylan introduces the copies of the faked canceled checks into evidence. "Where did Mr. Nash say he got these?"

"From Theresa Minardo. She worked for Mr. Oliva as a fundraiser."

"Were the lawsuits ultimately withdrawn?"

"Yes."

"Why was that done?"

"The paper publicly apologized for the error, and Mr. Nash's employment was terminated."

"Thank you. No further questions."

I begin my cross-examination by asking if any other

situation like this has happened in the twenty-seven years that Vince has been editor.

"No. Like everyone else, we've gotten some stories wrong, mostly in minor ways, but normally we've discovered it ourselves and ran retractions."

"So you were surprised when this happened?"

Hoffman nods. "Very."

"The original story contained no on-the-record sources, just anonymous. Correct?"

"Yes. Mr. Nash said that he promised his source it would be off-the-record. She insisted that her anonymity be preserved."

"When Mr. Minchner and Mayor Oliva provided their proof that the story was wrong, did Mr. Nash then reveal his source?"

"Yes. There was no longer any reason to protect her. Mr. Nash said she had not lived up to her side of the bargain."

"That was Ms. Minardo?"

"Yes. And she denied having had anything to do with the story or providing the documents to Mr. Nash."

"Were you surprised that Mr. Nash went with a story that could be so easily disproven?"

Hoffman nods. "Very much so. It made no sense to me. And to identify Ms. Minardo as the source, if in fact she wasn't and would deny everything, was also puzzling in the extreme. It was not a smart thing to do if he was trying to be deceptive, and Mr. Nash is an intelligent young man."

"Do you think Ms. Minardo was lying when she said she was not the source of the story?"

Hoffman pauses for a few moments. "I think Mr. Nash was telling the truth."

"You mean you think the story was true?"

"No, but I believe that he thought it was. That's just my opinion. I can't speak to Ms. Minardo's actions or motives, and at this point, the circumstances being what they are, I wouldn't want to anyway."

"I understand. Thank you."

Dylan's next witness is Jean Martone. She is a former colleague of Bobby's at the newspaper, though she has since left that business and gone back to school.

By her demeanor she is the definition of a reluctant witness; she and Bobby were and are friends, and she clearly hates testifying against him.

Dylan establishes that friendship, punctuated by the revelation that Bobby was at her wedding. Then, "Did you have occasion to speak to Mr. Nash approximately one week before the murders?"

She nods. "Yes. We had dinner at the Bonfire."

"Did the incident with the story about Mayor Oliva and Richard Minchner come up?"

"Yes. Bobby talked about it a lot. He had lost his job because of it."

"He was still upset about it, even though it had been a few months?"

"Yes."

"Did he specifically mention Mayor Oliva and Theresa Minardo at any point?"

She looks over at Bobby, unhappy to be saying these things. "Yes."

"What did he say about them?"

"Well, Ms. Minardo, he said that she'd lied, that she was the source of the story and then denied it. He also somehow thought that it was prearranged, and that Mayor Oliva was in on it. He also included Mr. Minchner in that."

"Did he think they did all that to somehow hurt him?"

"I don't think so, but I don't know. He said he was trying to get to the bottom of it."

"Did he say what he meant by 'getting to the bottom of it'?"

"No."

Dylan turns her over to me, and I ask, "Ms. Martone, when you had this conversation, did you consider calling the police?"

She looks surprised. "No. Why would I do that?"

"To protect Mr. Oliva and Ms. Minardo. Didn't you think he might turn violent and hurt them?"

"Absolutely not. That's not Bobby . . . Mr. Nash."

"So Mr. Nash was angry at Ms. Minardo because she provided the documents and the story to him and then denied it? He said that she lied about it and hung him out to dry?"

"Yes. He might even have used those exact words."

"Let me offer a hypothetical. Let's imagine for a moment that the story was not only false, but that Ms. Minardo had nothing to do with it, as she claimed. In this hypothetical, she had no contact with Mr. Nash and never gave him the documents. Mr. Nash just made the whole thing up. Understand?"

"Yes."

"So here's the question. Under this hypothetical, if Mr. Nash made it all up and never had contact with Ms. Minardo in the first place, why would he hold a grudge against her? Why would he be angry with her for refusing to admit providing the documents, if she actually hadn't provided them in the first place?"

"Well, I guess he wouldn't; he'd have no reason to blame her in that case. She would have been just telling the truth, and he would have known that."

"Exactly. And in that same hypothetical, that the story was false and that Mr. Nash made it up, why would he be angry with the mayor? The mayor would have just been defending himself from a false story, correct?"

Martone can't conceal a small smile. "Yes. Correct."

"So it would only make sense for Mr. Nash to hold a grudge against these people if the story was actually true, right? If it was true, then they were lying, and he'd have reason to be angry, wouldn't he?"

"Yes."

"But the story was proven false, was it not?"

"I believe that it was."

"Thank you. No further questions."

When I get back to the defense table, Bobby leans over and says, "That was really smart."

"Aww, shucks."

When I leave the court for the day, as I'm getting into my car, the phone rings and it's Pete Stanton. "You coming to Charlie's tonight?"

"I hadn't planned on it."

"Come to Charlie's. I want to talk to you."

"Will Vince be there?"

Pete laughs. "Vince? No chance; there's a thirty-percent-off sale at Petco. He'll be shopping."

"Okay. I'll see you there."

I'm reasonably pleased with how today's court session went, though we were helped by Dylan's inexplicably starting with two reluctant witnesses.

In any event, it doesn't really matter; Dylan's case will not rise or fall on motive evidence. That is merely a setup, a preamble. He's got powerful weapons to use at his convenience whenever he's ready to drop the hammer.

I still believe that Minchner is behind everything that happened, and Jerry Conti is behind Minchner. I'm not sure what the two of them gained by Oliva's death, but they obviously considered him a danger.

Possibly his being the favorite for governor caused them to panic and kill him. The ironic aspect is Nancy Oliva's revelation that he had changed his mind and was not going to run for governor. Had he not kept that a secret, he might be alive today.

I have a quick dinner with Laurie, then I spend some time playing video football with Ricky. The next time I beat him at a video game will be the first. I might consider deliberately letting him win, as a considerate and loving fatherly gesture, but that decision has never been necessary, since he kicks my ass every single time.

Someday, sometime, I will get my revenge.

After a quick walk with the dogs, I head down to Charlie's. There's some good NBA basketball on tonight, but I could watch that at home. I'm going because Pete asked me to.

When I get there, I see that Vince's regular seat is occupied, but not by Vince. Pete and whoever this newcomer is must have just gotten here, because menus are still on the table. Pete, since he eats here every night, obviously doesn't need a menu, but the other guy does.

Pete introduces him as Lieutenant Charlie Briggs, who he says is a New Jersey state cop in the organized crime division. Briggs comes off as a tough, no-nonsense cop. That is not my favorite; I generally prefer the weak, nonsense types.

The waiter comes over and Briggs picks up the menu. "Order whatever you want," Pete advises, "it's on Andy."

Briggs nods. "How is the New York–cut sirloin?"

The waiter says, "Excellent. But the filet is even better."

"Perfect. I'll have two of those."

The waiter doesn't bother to ask Pete and me what we want, since we have the same thing every time—a burger, burnt french fries, and a light beer. I'm not a big fan of beer, but it feels like a sacrilege not to have one in a sports bar.

"So you called me here so that I can buy you losers dinner?" I ask.

"Of course not," Pete says. "Don't insult me. It would have gone on your tab whether you were here or not."

"So why am I here?"

"Drew Churasick. I've been checking on him since you mentioned him."

"Good."

Briggs says, "Those two guys you had the run-in with, one of whom is now in that crime family in the sky, worked under Churasick. Who in turn works for Jerry Conti."

"Tell me something I don't know."

"Churasick is in town, or at least he was a few days ago."

"Tell me something I don't know."

"He met with Joseph Russo."

Briggs just hit on something I didn't know, but which doesn't surprise me.

Briggs continues, "We had Junior under surveillance and Churasick showed up. The cop didn't know who he was, but got a photo of him. It's definitely Churasick." Junior is the name commonly used for Russo, since he took over the family from Joseph Russo, Sr., who had his head blown off.

I just nod, and Briggs continues, "Now you tell me something I don't know."

"Churasick killed Alex Oliva and Theresa Minardo."

Pete frowns. "Andy is representing the real killer, so take that for what it's worth."

"This is not supposition. He was there; I'll be able to prove it at trial. If he didn't do the killings, then it's an amazing coincidence that he was there to observe."

"How do you know this?" Pete asks.

"I can't say, but you'll see at trial."

"Is this your friend Sam with that phone GPS thing?"

"Sam would never do anything illegal. He wouldn't jay-walk." I turn to Briggs. "I knew his phone number, but he apparently ditched it. I can tell you the fake ID he flew here under and used to rent a car, but I don't know where he is."

"Let me have the name."

I take out one of my cards and write *Ronald Devers* on it and hand it to him. "Here you go."

"Since you seem to know so much," Briggs says, "what do you know about the bombing at the bus station?"

Just his asking the question feels hugely significant. I haven't thought about a connection between the bus station and our case because there seems to be no logic behind it. Also, Corey told me that a different type of explosive was used. "Is Churasick part of that?"

"His specialty in the army was explosives and ordnance, but at this point we have no reason to connect him to it."

"What could the motive be?" I ask. "Conti is not a terrorist; he's into profit. How could they profit from blowing up an empty bus station?"

"That is not clear," Briggs says.

I then ask, "Why would Churasick be meeting with Junior?"

"Because Conti must have wanted him to; Churasick does nothing on his own. And Conti must have wanted him to because Conti is moving in here."

"And Junior is okay with that?"

"Seems to be."

"Does he have a choice?" I ask.

"Probably does; Conti would not want to fight a war on foreign soil. But you can be sure it will be mutually beneficial. Conti brings manpower and money."

"But why here? What is there about this area that appeals to Conti? Aren't there more target-rich environments?"

Briggs nods. "You would think so, but Conti wouldn't be doing it without a reason. A very good reason."

The waiter brings over our food, placing the burgers and fries in front of Pete and me, and the two filets in front of Briggs.

Briggs cuts into one of them and takes a bite. He turns to the waiter. "This is excellent. I'm going to need another one of these."

Dylan makes what I consider another surprising decision and calls Nancy Oliva as his first witness today.

I suppose he had little choice, and this is the least of two evils for him. He now knows that she has her doubts that it was Bobby who made those threatening phone calls about her husband. But since those doubts were going to come out anyway in the defense case, he wants to be the one to reveal them and portray them in the light most favorable to the prosecution.

After identifying Nancy as Alex Oliva's widow, Dylan tells her how sorry he is for her loss. I'm sure he has had ample opportunity to do so before and no doubt did, but he wants to do it in front of the jury, so they will see what a caring and empathetic guy he is.

Then he gets down to the nitty-gritty. "Mrs. Oliva, did you receive two phone calls from a man who identified himself as Bobby Nash?"

"Yes."

"Was that on the day that your husband was killed?"

"One was the day before, and one was on the actual day."

"He called at your home?"

"Yes."

"What did he say each time?"

"Both times were generally the same, and I certainly don't remember the exact words. But basically he was angry, and he said that Alex had ruined his life, and he insisted on meeting with Alex, so that he could 'deal with this.'"

"He definitely used the words *deal with this*?"

She nods. "Yes. That much I clearly remember."

"Did you take these calls as a threat? Did they worry you?"

"Yes."

"Did you tell your husband about them?"

"I did, and I told him I thought he should tell the police. He didn't want to because of the publicity if the word got out, but he was considering it."

"Later on, weeks after that day, did you come to question whether in fact it was Mr. Nash who made the calls?"

"Yes."

"Why was that?"

"Well, I was surprised that he called at home, and not Alex's office. And it was our private number, so I don't know how he would have gotten it. But mostly it was because I saw an interview on television that Mr. Nash did, and the voice did not sound the same."

"The voice on the phone was angry, but the voice on the television was not, is that correct?"

"Yes."

"And one voice was through a phone line, and the other was not, true?"

"True."

"Thank you, no further questions."

It was well done by Dylan; he defused her doubts by

bringing them out himself and showing that the prosecution has nothing to hide.

My first question is, "Mrs. Oliva, what was your profession when you married Alex Oliva?"

"I was a speech therapist."

"Did you have a degree in speech therapy?"

"Yes. A master's from the University of Washington."

"Do you consider yourself an expert at recognizing differences in voices, their inflections, their tones?"

"I did."

"Not anymore?"

She thinks for a moment. "I believe I am, yes."

"Is your training such that the quality and identity of the voice can be determined regardless of whether the person is angry or not?"

"I believe so, yes."

"Or whether it is heard through a phone or a television?"

"Certainly, yes."

"At the time you received those calls, you had never heard Mr. Nash's voice, had you?"

"I had not."

"So you had nothing to compare it to?"

"That is correct."

"And today you are confident that it was not Mr. Nash's voice you heard that day?"

"I am now. I wish I'd realized it then."

"When your husband was killed, you immediately told the police about the phone calls because you thought they might be relevant. Is that correct?"

"Yes. In my mind, Alex was threatened and then he was killed. It was an obvious connection for me to make."

"Are you aware that one of the main reasons the police arrested Mr. Nash so quickly was because you told them of the threatening calls?"

Dylan jumps out of his seat like it was on fire and objects that it was beyond the scope of the direct testimony and that she could not place herself in the mind of the police.

Judge Koenig sustains and tells the jury to disregard the question, then says, "You know better than that, Mr. Carpenter."

I do know better, and the other thing I know is that the jury will not be able to unhear the question, and they will know that the police rushed to arrest Bobby on information that the provider of that information considers false.

"Sorry, Your Honor. No further questions."

The afternoon session begins with Dylan starting to get into the meat of his case.

What I would consider the more difficult areas for him to navigate, the motive testimony and that of Nancy Oliva, are behind him. I think we've been able to counter it pretty well, but nothing that has been said so far will carry the day.

The heavy artillery is coming.

I notice for the first time that James Pritchett, assistant or executive or whatever for Richard Minchner, is in the gallery watching. He may have been here for the previous testimony as well, but I didn't notice one way or the other.

One thing I have no doubt about is that Minchner will be interested in every aspect of these proceedings. I'm sure that Pritchett will describe the events in great detail. I'm going to see to it that Minchner has reason to be interested.

It begins after the lunch break with Sergeant Stew Metofsky of the Paterson Police Department. He and his partner were the first to arrive on the scene at Eastside Park in response to my call after Tara dug up the mayor's hand.

"We received a notification through Captain Stanton of homicide; he had been made aware that a body was discovered in the park. My partner and I were the first to arrive on the scene."

"What did you find when you got there?"

"Mr. Carpenter and another man, David Divine, were there with three dogs. They said that they had been walking the dogs when one of them detected something in the snow. The dog apparently dug into the snow with his paws, revealing the hand of the deceased. The remainder of the body was covered by a fairly deep snow, perhaps nine inches."

"What did you do then?"

"I felt for a pulse, determined there was none, and then my partner and I secured the area and waited for homicide and forensics to arrive, which they did within ten minutes."

"When did you realize that the victim was Mayor Oliva?"

"I was told about an hour after we arrived."

Dylan turns the witness over to me. Metofsky has not done us any damage at all, so ordinarily I would not need to ask him any significant questions. I am slightly troubled, though, by my introduction to the case itself, regarding my discovery of the body.

"Sergeant Metofsky, are you aware that I live only eight blocks from the park?"

"I know you mentioned that in your statement."

"Are you aware that I walk my dogs in that park almost every night?"

"Again, I just know it was in your statement."

"Are you aware that I was not Mr. Nash's attorney at the time the body was discovered?"

"I was not aware of that, no."

"Was there anything that happened, or that you saw, to cause you to question Mr. Divine's and my description of the events that night?"

"There was not."

"Thank you, no further questions."

Dylan next calls Sergeant Pamela Duckmanton, also of the Paterson PD. Sergeant Duckmanton and her partner were the first to arrive at the mayor's house after Nancy Oliva called 911 the night of the murder.

"Sergeant Duckmanton, you were responding to a nine-one-one call from Mrs. Oliva?"

"That's right. I . . ."

She stops talking because a bailiff enters the courtroom and walks over to Judge Koenig. This rarely if ever happens during testimony, and it surprises Sergeant Duckmanton, as it does the rest of us.

Judge Koenig explains the interruption, at least partially. "Ladies and gentlemen, we have a security situation here. Everyone needs to leave the building in an orderly fashion out through the rear door. Please assemble in the street and wait for instructions. Jurors, please follow the bailiff and stay together. A bailiff will escort the defendant as well. Let's do this calmly and quickly."

It all happens with remarkable efficiency. I tell Eddie to go out the rear door, but I stay with Bobby and go along with the bailiff as we go out a side door and into an alleyway. A van is waiting there, and the bailiff, who I know from trying many cases here, says, "Sorry, Andy. No lawyers allowed."

I won't get anywhere arguing the point, so as they put Bobby into the van, I head down the alley to go around toward the front of the building. One of the first people I see is Dylan.

"What's going on?" I ask.

"A bomb went off at an American Legion Hall on Market Street; two people were killed and at least a dozen injured."

"So why did that send us out into the street?"

"I'm told, and don't quote me on this, that there were bomb scares called into the courthouse and City Hall."

I nod. "That explains that."

Then police start to move everyone farther and farther away, and I see bomb squad vehicles pull up to the building. There is no question that bomb scares are to be taken seriously when actual bombs are going off in the city.

It's getting late in the day, and I can't imagine court will resume today, but I don't feel like I can head home. Finally, a bailiff spots us in the crowd and tells us it's okay to leave, that Judge Koenig has said that he hopes to reconvene tomorrow.

"Did they find anything inside?" I ask.

The bailiff shakes his head. "No, but they're still looking. It's a big building."

Every major newscast leads with the situation in Paterson.

This is far from the norm, since Paterson is in what is called the New York DMA, which means that we get the local New York stations. Since that covers the entire metropolitan area, it's rare that Paterson has news considered worthy of being covered.

Covering this story is a no-brainer.

One thing that comes across loud and clear is that the police have no suspects. The standard appeal is being put out for anyone with information to call a tip line. They seem to be floundering so badly that I'm surprised the tip-line number isn't 1–800–WE DON'T HAVE A CLUE.

Another obvious development, revealed in street interviews, is that the citizens of Paterson are becoming very concerned, if not panicked. The first bomb bothered people, but it seemed to be an isolated case, so not a cause for great alarm. This second bombing, along with the phoned-in scares, has upped the ante considerably.

Acting Mayor Womack holds a press conference, during which his frustration with the lack of progress and with the police commissioner, Randy Bauer, is evident. This view of Bauer might well be colored by the rivalry between them, as Bauer remains Womack's main competition for mayor in November.

But even though they are claiming that this investigation is in the early stages, it has really been ongoing since the bus station bombing, and they are getting nowhere. Womack has had enough, and his frustration is understandable, especially since his election prospects could be tied into his success or failure in bringing the perpetrators to justice:

"I have today called upon both the FBI and ATF to take control of the investigation into both today's bombing and the bus station bombing a few weeks ago, in conjunction with the New Jersey State Police. I have instructed Commissioner Bauer to commit the resources of the Paterson Police Department to aid them in their efforts, in whatever way they see fit.

"Those agencies have agreed to our request and are mobilizing to deal with this emergency now. Paterson is not going to be held hostage to violence and terrorism; we are going to show the toughness and resilience that is our history, and we will not back down.

"Thank you."

Laurie says, "He just dug Bauer's political grave and shoveled dirt on him. It was quite a performance."

"For sure. He dumped on Bauer and then turned it over to the Feds. If they can't solve it, or stop it, the blame doesn't land directly on him. Womack is a better politician than I thought."

"Does all this affect our case?"

"Well, it delayed it a few hours, which is a plus. But other than that, I can't imagine how. It's hard to see how the trial was a target for this, any more than City Hall was. They're just prominent government buildings so they got threatened, but they are not where the bombs went off."

"You have any idea who could be doing this?"

I shake my head. "None. When the state cop, Briggs, mentioned Churasick, I thought maybe he might be involved, that Conti could be making a play for something. But I don't know what it could be; there is no profit to be made in random bombings and threats. Conti is evil, but he's not a terrorist. He's a businessman."

"No way to tie any of the bombings to the one that killed Theresa Minardo? Or even to raise the possibility?"

"No. I wish there was. Corey found out that a different type of explosive was used, and a different type of device. Hers was set off by activating the garage door opener. The bus station was triggered by a cell phone call. I haven't heard yet how they did the American Legion Hall, but there seems no way for me to make the connection to Minardo. At least not yet."

With all the stress that has gone on, I want tonight to be normal and relaxing. I take the dogs for a walk, and I am happy when Ricky wants to go with me.

We talk about school, and his friends, and football. It is the kind of thing I too rarely get to do during a trial; in fact, it's the kind of thing I too rarely get to do in life.

As we walk, I'm thinking that Ricky is growing up fast. Before I know it, he'll be a full-fledged teenager who will basically want nothing to do with me. Then he'll be in college, and I'll only see him occasionally. Even worse, with him out of the house I'll have to go back to picking out and decorating the Christmas tree with Laurie.

"You know, Rick, maybe you should go to a local college and commute."

"I thought you wanted me to go to Michigan and play football?"

"I'm rethinking it."

When I get home, Laurie tells me that the court clerk called, and that the trial will resume tomorrow morning.

I'm not surprised by that, and certainly not pleased.

But at least I got to walk and talk with Ricky.

Sergeant Duckmanton is back on the stand as court begins.

When the bomb scare happened, she had just started her testimony about arriving at the Olivas' house the night of the murder.

Dylan starts his direct examination with "As we were saying . . ." He says it with a smile; it's his version of a joke, even though he has the sense of humor of an overturned tractor trailer.

This one must have been slipped to him by a backup humor lawyer, because it goes over pretty well. The gallery laughs and the jury smiles; albeit all a bit nervously.

He waits for the reaction to subside and then adds, "You were responding to a nine-one-one call from Mrs. Oliva?"

"Yes. She had called because she had been out to dinner, and when she got home, she saw that the rear door to their house was ajar. That was extremely unusual, and she was worried."

"Was her husband, Mayor Oliva, not at home?"

"He was not. She expected that; he was scheduled to be at a political dinner, so she did not realize that anything had happened to him."

"What did you do when you arrived?"

"My partner and I went to the rear of the house to see what she was talking about. I asked her to turn the outside lights on, and when she did, I noticed what could possibly be blood near the garage."

I called to my partner to come over to observe it, and Mrs. Oliva heard me and did as well. It was then that she looked through the window of the garage and noticed Mayor Oliva's car was still there."

"What happened next?"

"Mrs. Oliva became extremely upset; she said he had definitely planned to drive. My partner took her inside the house while I called in backup support, detectives, and forensics. By that point I was quite sure it was blood on the ground.

"At that point a few neighbors, I would say half a dozen, had gathered at the end of the driveway. I don't know if it was our squad cars or Mrs. Oliva's cries that had drawn them, but I made sure that no one approached the scene until other officers arrived.

"Another patrol car arrived quickly and I let those officers deal with the neighbors while I went inside to join my partner and Mrs. Oliva."

"I assume she was still upset?"

"Very. She was positive that something bad had happened to him, even though I hadn't told her that what I had seen on the ground was blood."

"Why was she so sure? If all she knew was that his car was there, couldn't he have gotten a ride to the event?"

"Two reasons, the least of which was that she was trying to call him on his cell, but only getting voice mail. The main reason was that she had described getting threatening phone calls that day and the day before from Mr. Nash."

Most of what Sergeant Duckmanton has said are basic facts and not damaging to us. So there is little for me to challenge.

The last part, where she mentioned Bobby, is a double-edged sword. Dylan has not shied away from it, which means I have to counter it each time.

"Sergeant Duckmanton, you said that Mrs. Oliva mentioned that she had received threatening phone calls from Mr. Nash," I say when it's my turn to question her.

"Yes."

"Are you aware that she testified in this trial that she had changed her mind, that she now believes it was not Mr. Nash?"

"I am aware of that."

"Are you aware that she possessed a master's degree in speech therapy?"

"Yes. I have since become aware of that."

"Thank you. No further questions."

New York State officer Gerritt Lowry is next up. He is a setup witness, meaning that he will just be presenting some incontrovertible facts to set the table for future witnesses.

Lowry is the officer called to the scene of Bobby's car crash, in a ditch off the Palisades Interstate Parkway. The Palisades is one of the few highways that goes north from New Jersey to New York without crossing the Hudson River.

Bobby crashed in a ditch north of the New York line, which is why the New York State cops handled it.

That the car was found at all, or at least as quickly as it was, was a complete fluke. Another car pulled over right nearby with a flat tire, and when the driver got out, he looked down the hill and thought he saw a light. It was the taillight of Bobby's car, down a steep ditch. It could have been there for a long while without being discovered, had that flat tire not occurred.

As Dylan is drawing this out of Lowry, my eyes wander to the jury and then the gallery. Everybody seems a bit on edge this morning; there's an energy that hasn't been there since the opening statements. I think it must have been the bomb scare yesterday; it's had an effect on all of us, me included. It's all everyone in town is talking about, so the people in the courtroom would not be an exception.

"Officer Lowry, what did you do when you arrived on the scene?"

"I worked my way down into the ditch to see exactly what was going on. At the same time I called in for backup and alerted the dispatcher that a rescue squad might be necessary."

"Why did you do that?"

"I could tell from the position of the car that if there was a driver in it, I would never be able to get him up the hill by myself, even if he was not badly injured. I had my doubts that I could get back up myself. My partner waited at the top to direct the people that would arrive."

Dylan introduces various pictures of the scene, including those taken from the road and up close. "What did you find when you got there?"

"The car was banged up, though not as bad as I would have expected. It had landed with the front still facing forward and the windshield cracked. I assumed that the driver's head had hit it."

"Was the driver in the car, and if so, was it Mr. Nash?"

"Yes and yes."

"What was his condition?"

"He was unconscious and completely unresponsive. He had a pulse, but it was very faint."

"Were you able to extricate him from the car?"

"No chance. I didn't try. The rescue people did that, they have the tools required. Then Mr. Nash was taken off in a chopper."

My first question is to refer to one of the photos taken from the road and ask if it looks like the shrubbery was crushed all along the hill going down.

Lowry nods. "Yes, it was. I was aware of that as I made my way down."

"So the car didn't have loft when it left the road?"

"Not sure what you mean."

"Well, if you're driving at a high speed when you get to the edge of a cliff, you don't go straight down, do you? Don't you soar in the air a bit until gravity takes hold?"

"Yes, I would think so."

"But that didn't happen here. It seems like the car just rolled down the hill, through the shrubbery, doesn't it?"

"Probably, yes. But I couldn't say for sure."

"Wouldn't that also explain why you said the car had less damage than you would have thought?"

"It could."

"You said that the driver was in the car, and you said that was Mr. Nash."

"Right."

"Did you ever see him driving that car?"

"Well . . . no. Not at the point I was there."

"So just based on your observations, you don't know if he was the driver, you just know he was in the driver's seat when you found him. Is that correct?"

"I made an assumption."

"I'm sure you did," I say. "But I'm not asking about your assumptions, I'm asking about what you actually saw."

"Then, yes, I only saw him in the driver's seat."

"Thank you."

Dylan's next witness is Dr. Joann Temple, an emergency room physician at St. Joseph's Hospital. That is where Bobby was taken by helicopter from the scene. I'm surprised they went there; I would have thought Hackensack Hospital was closer and a more logical choice.

My strong belief is that the police were involved in that decision because Bobby was already the main suspect in the mayor's death.

Dylan is going through witnesses at a rapid pace. It's unusual for him; he usually takes an hour to do what he could do in fifteen minutes. He must be anxious to get to the juicy stuff.

Dr. Temple describes Bobby's condition when he arrived. Physically he had sustained a severe concussion, a number of broken bones, and cracked ribs.

"And you tested his blood?" Dylan asks.

"Of course."

"What did you find that might be described as unusual?"

"There was a high level of fentanyl, mixed with a lower level of alcohol."

"When you say 'high level,' what do you mean by that?"

"Well, to be honest, it is a dose that very often could be lethal. That level easily could have killed him, independent of any injuries sustained in the crash."

Dylan shows her the toxicologist's report, which basically describes the fentanyl level in the same way, and asks if Dr. Temple agrees with his assessment. Of course she does.

Dr. Temple goes on to describe how she and her team stabilized him, kept his failing organs functioning, and ultimately brought him to consciousness. There is no question in my mind that their heroic efforts saved his life.

I decline to cross-examine; I have points I can make, but I can more effectively make them with other witnesses.

Today was not a terrible day; tomorrow will be a lot worse.

I t is no wonder that the police have not been able to catch the bomber. They've spent all their time testifying at this trial.

Patrolman Donald Harrison was one of the first officers on the scene at Theresa Minardo's house after the explosion. He's not a significant witness at all, other than that he's the first one to bring the Theresa Minardo death into the trial.

All of the fact witnesses have so far been related to Mayor Oliva, so Dylan is just checking a box with Patrolman Harrison.

Harrison describes the damage he found when he arrived, and Dylan supplements it with photographs. Fortunately there are no photographs of the charred body of Minardo in the burned-out wreckage, but it is still horrifying to everyone watching that a person could have been trapped in this.

Harrison describes what it was like finding the body. "The wreckage of the car was still charred and burning, but I could see that there was no possibility that she was still alive."

"Have you ever dealt with a situation like that before?" Dylan asks.

"No, and I hope I never have to again. It was horrible."

When it's my turn, I refer to the photographs, but not of the wreckage itself. My focus is on the surrounding houses and yards. "Patrolman Harrison, you said you checked the surrounding area to see if by any chance the perpetrator was still there."

"Yes. There was always a chance that he could have accidentally got caught in the blast and was injured. Or maybe stayed behind to watch his handiwork."

I point to the adjacent areas in the various directions from the garage and ask if he looked there. Each time he answers, "Yes."

Once he's done that, I point to the area behind the house, backing onto the street. He's already said that he checked that area, but I ask him to repeat it. When he does, I ask, "So you believed that it was possible the perpetrator had come from this area?"

"Yes."

"Hypothetically, the perpetrator could have parked on that street, gone through that alley to the back of Ms. Minardo's garage, and set the explosive device?"

"It seemed possible."

"And still does?"

"Yes."

I let Harrison off the stand, pleased with the testimony, since I am going to submit the GPS evidence in our defense case showing that Churasick, or at least his phone, was on that street. Dylan doesn't know about it yet because I haven't subpoenaed the records, so he probably can't figure out the purpose of my questioning.

He will soon enough.

Yesterday we served a subpoena on Richard Minchner requiring his testimony during our case. Our server said he was pissed off to receive it, but that is certainly not an unheard-of attitude among subpoena recipients.

I'm about to learn more about his reaction because as we're leaving the courthouse, I see James Pritchett, Minchner's right-hand person, approaching me. He has been here every day of the trial, or at least every day since I first noticed him.

Pritchett does not seem too happy to see me; we haven't developed the warm, close-knit relationship I generally have with adversaries during a case.

"Mr. Carpenter, I want to talk with you."

I nod. "And I will 'consent' to talk with you." I'm still annoyed that he used that language the first time I set up a meeting with his boss. I expect I will at some point mature, but right now that doesn't seem imminent.

I take him back to an anteroom that we use for client conferences. "The floor is yours," I say.

His attitude seems different, less arrogant, and his words reflect it. "Mr. Carpenter, I think you are smart enough to know that I deliver messages, I don't send them and I don't create them."

"Doesn't absolve you of blame. You could quit your job and go to work for a non-asshole."

"That's not as easy as you think; I wish it was. But I have a message to deliver."

"Then by all means go for it."

"Okay. Mr. Minchner was extremely unhappy that he was subpoenaed to testify. He says that he has nothing to do with this case, and he will not obey the subpoena."

I laugh. "Good luck with that."

"He isn't laughing. He also does not want his relationship with Ms. Minardo to become public knowledge, and he denies it."

"He's zero for two so far. You got anything else?"

Pritchett looks severely stressed. "Mr. Carpenter, please understand who you are dealing with. Minchner has friends, powerful friends who I won't name, who will not let you poke around in their lives. You can get through this trial without implicating him, and you should do that."

"Maybe I can, or maybe not. But I won't."

"I'm not here to warn you. I'm here to give you the message, that's all. I hope you take it seriously."

I smile. "How are you liking the trial so far?"

"I'm biased. But you're very good at what you do."

"You're not so bad yourself."

When I get home, I tell Laurie about the conversation with Pritchett, and the implied threat that he was delivering about how Minchner's "powerful friends" might react to my actions.

"They've tried to kill you once, and Bobby as well, so this is unwelcome, but not a surprise."

"Do you still have Marcus watching out for me?"

"Yes."

"Good. If we knew where Churasick was, I might suggest we go on the offensive, but we don't."

She nods. "So until we find him, we remain careful. And after we find him, we still remain careful."

Lieutenant Brad Pierce walking to the stand indicates we are moving into the next phase of the trial.

Dylan has set the table and is now preparing to bombard the jury with what he considers more than they'll need to put Bobby away. Lieutenant Pierce is a key, maybe the main one, to accomplishing that.

Pierce took over the investigation from the moment he showed up at Eastside Park. As a homicide detective he reports to Pete Stanton, who has supervised and been responsible for everything Pierce has done, but Pierce has been out front. Because of that, he's the obvious choice for Dylan to bring before the jury.

After taking Pierce through the progress of his career and the commendations he has received, Dylan turns to the specifics of the case. "Lieutenant, you supervised the crime scene at Eastside Park that night?"

"I did, reporting to Captain Stanton."

"Were you there when it was discovered that the victim was Mayor Oliva?"

"I was."

"What were your initial assumptions?"

"Well, it was clear that the cause of death was a gunshot

wound in his back. But I realized early on that the shooting did not take place there, that the body was moved."

"What made you say that?"

"The lack of blood. I would have expected much more, and it would have been spattered. Though the snow made things a bit more difficult, it seemed to me that the body was placed there."

"Did forensics ultimately confirm that?"

"Yes, sir."

Dylan asked him to relate his actions after that, and Pierce says that it obviously tied into a report they had gotten about the situation at the mayor's house. "We went there and immediately understood that the shooting had taken place there. Among other reasons, there was blood spatter on the side of the garage, and a substantial amount of blood on the ground. All of it was consistent with the type of wound that the mayor suffered."

"And your attention quickly turned to Mr. Nash. Why was that?"

"Well, first of all, Mrs. Oliva described threatening phone calls from him. Then we received a report that Mr. Nash's car had crashed into a ditch, and that there was significant blood in the trunk. Also a neighbor of the mayor had noticed a car parked at an odd angle on the street in a no-parking area. He took down the license plate; it was Mr. Nash's car."

"The car he ultimately drove into the ditch?"

"Yes."

"So a combination of factors led to the arrest?"

"Yes, though we didn't technically arrest him at first. He was unconscious, so we were unable to read him his rights. We took him into custody, and he remained at the hospital under guard."

"The defense has referred to the speed with which you made the arrest of Mr. Nash—or took him into custody—as a rush to judgment. Is that how you see it?"

"No, we make arrests when we think the evidence justifies it; the timing is never a factor."

"You are aware that Mrs. Oliva no longer believes it was Mr. Nash who made those calls?"

"Yes."

"Had she not mentioned the phone calls at all, would you still have taken Mr. Nash into custody?"

"Yes, definitely. Perhaps not quite as quickly, but once the blood in his trunk was identified as the mayor's, that would have clinched it. We're talking about a couple of hours' difference, which didn't matter because he was unconscious in the hospital anyway."

"Did you also supervise the investigation into Ms. Minardo's death?"

"I did."

"What led you to the conclusion that Mr. Nash was the perpetrator?"

"Well, there was motive, obviously; he had publicly expressed significant bitterness toward her. But that alone would not have been enough. Then traces of the type of explosives used were subsequently found in his basement, and that clinched it in our minds."

"Thank you. No further questions."

Pierce has done, as expected, a great deal of damage, and we have to combat some of it.

"Lieutenant Pierce, you believed Mrs. Oliva when she told you about threatening calls from Mr. Nash, correct?"

"Yes, of course."

"You consider her an honest person?"

"I have no reason not to."

"And you believe that today she thinks it was not Mr. Nash, correct?"

He nods. "Yes, I do."

"And you believe her when she says she has a master's in speech therapy, had a private practice in that field, and is an expert?"

"Yes."

"Do you think she is correct in her revised view?"

"I don't know; I never heard the phone calls."

"So she could be right, or perhaps not. Is that how you feel about it?"

"Yes."

"So if you're not sure either way, then it follows that it's reasonable to think she might be right or she might be wrong?"

The word *reasonable* is a charged in a trial because of reasonable doubt, but he has no choice but to accept it here. "Yes."

"Now, I want to offer a hypothetical. Since she might be right and might be wrong, suppose for the purpose of this hypothetical that she's right, that it wasn't Mr. Nash that called. Will you do that?"

"Yes."

"If it wasn't Mr. Nash, then it would be true that someone else threatened Mayor Oliva on the day he was killed, as well as the day before. Is that something that would interest you as an investigator?"

He's trapped. I would say that I like trapping witnesses more than watching Super Bowls. I admit that may reveal a character defect of mine.

"Yes. Of course we would be interested in that."

"Mrs. Oliva informed the prosecution four weeks ago that she no longer believes it was Mr. Nash that called, and you have said it is reasonable to think she might be right. So how is the new investigation going?"

"What new investigation?"

"Have you not commenced a new investigation to determine who actually made those calls?"

"We have not."

"Oh." I fake surprise at this revelation. "So you were interested in what she had to say, but not enough to look into it. Is that what you consider to be good, unbiased policing?"

Dylan objects and Judge Koenig strikes the question. Pierce looks pissed that I even asked it.

"Let's move on," I say. "Lieutenant Pierce, you said that the shooting of Mayor Oliva took place at his house, and his body was then left in Eastside Park. How far is the house from the park?"

"Three blocks."

"Why do you think the body was moved? Do you have a theory on that?"

"I couldn't say."

"Did the killer make an effort to hide the body so that it might never be found or not found for a long time? Or did he leave it thirty feet from a road in a public park?"

"It was left in Eastside Park," Pierce says, which is basically a nonanswer.

"According to the coroner's report, Mayor Oliva weighed

two hundred and ten pounds. Mr. Nash obviously is much smaller than that. Why would he pick up a large body like that, put it in his trunk, and drive three blocks? Why not just leave it where it was and take off? The blood spatter was there anyway."

"I don't know."

"Could it be to make sure that the mayor's blood and trace evidence of his clothing was found in the trunk?"

"I have no evidence of that at all."

"Was Mayor Oliva's blood found on Mr. Nash's clothing?"

"Not to my knowledge."

"You're the lead detective. Would you have that knowledge if it was found?"

"Yes."

"So Mr. Nash picked up the body of a man much larger than him, who had just been shot and bled profusely, and loaded him into the trunk of his car without getting blood on himself?"

"I assume he was careful."

I smile my disdain for his answer. "Yes, a man whose body was filled with drugs and alcohol, so much that he soon became unconscious and drove into a ditch, murdered a man and then suddenly became really careful. Is that what you believe, Lieutenant?"

Before he can answer, I shake my head in fake amazement at his testimony. "Never mind. No further questions."

I then turn and ask Judge Koenig to remind Lieutenant Pierce that he is subject to recall in the defense case; we are probably going to be calling him as a witness. Maybe I should have gone easier on him. Oops.

Richard Minchner took a deep breath before he made the call.

He had not dialed this number in a long time, not since arrangements were originally set. He was taking a chance by calling, but he felt it was a bigger risk not to call.

The phone was answered on the second ring. There was no greeting of any kind. Jerry Conti simply said, "Why are you not going through normal channels?"

"Because this needs your direct involvement. Things are getting serious, and dangerous for me personally. That cannot be good for anyone."

Conti didn't say anything for almost thirty seconds, to the point where Minchner thought he might have hung up. He finally said, "What is your problem?"

"They're calling me to testify in the Nash trial. The lawyer, Carpenter, is trying to make me the fall guy."

"I am already aware of that."

The comment irritated Minchner, but he was far more scared of Conti than he was annoyed by him. "He also knows about my relationship with Theresa."

"Do you have any new information to share?"

"I didn't realize you knew all this."

"There is very little about this situation that I don't

know, but I understand your concern," Conti said, surprising Minchner. "I am already taking steps to eliminate the problem."

"What are they?"

"You don't need to know. You don't even want to know. Suffice it to say the matter will be resolved quickly, and your concerns will be fully addressed."

Click.

Minchner was holding a dead phone. The call went as well as could be expected, perhaps even better, but he was still dreading whatever resolution Conti was talking about.

Minchner put the phone down and turned on the television. Acting Mayor Womack was delivering daily, televised updates on the bombing investigation. Womack obviously wanted to convey that he was on top of things and in charge, but actually had little information to share.

But Minchner watched every day anyway; it was a situation he was very interested in.

'm not big on making lists, but if I were to list my least favorite witnesses, Sergeant Xavier Jennings would be on it.

It seems like Jennings has been handling the bulk of the Paterson police forensics assignments since New Jersey reported to King George III. He is knowledgeable, competent, unflappable, and has an excellent rapport with juries. He's also a great guy, and juries can immediately sense that.

I hate him.

But as the old saying sort of goes, you play the witnesses that you are dealt, so I resign myself to some pain when Dylan calls Jennings to the stand.

Probably recognizing that the Minardo murder is the weakest part of his case against Bobby, Dylan starts with that first, having Jennings describe the trace evidence of explosive that was found in Bobby's basement.

"It was Cintron 421," Jennings says, "a very powerful explosive. It's sometimes used to take down buildings and stadiums."

"And in this case all it had to do was take down Theresa Minardo's garage, with Theresa Minardo in it?"

"Yes, both our lab and the ATF confirmed its use on the Minardo garage."

"Is it possible the Cintron 421 trace was in the basement accidentally? Might it have appeared there without intent?"

"No. It's very rare, hard to procure, and complicated to make. It would not just show up in someone's house."

Moving to the Oliva killing, Dylan asks Jennings if the blood in the trunk of Bobby's car was definitely Oliva's.

"No question about it. It's his DNA; it would effectively be impossible for it not to be his. One in almost a quadrillion."

"And the same blood was found outside the mayor's house?"

"Yes."

"And can we assume that the fibers gathered from the car trunk were also consistent with what the mayor was wearing when he was shot?"

Jennings nods. "You would be right to assume that."

Dylan takes another half hour to go over basically the same material he has already covered, then turns the witness over to me. I start by introducing photographs taken at the time the search warrant was executed on Bobby's house. The photos are of both the inside and the outside, but I ask him to look at the one in the driveway.

"This is what it looked like when you arrived?" I ask.

"Yes."

"Look at this window, the one that is open. Did you or anyone you were with open it?"

"No."

"Did you examine it? Perhaps look for fingerprints on the window and windowsill?"

"No."

"Did you think it was unusual for one window in a house to be open, in late November?"

"I didn't think about it at all."

"Was there a burglar alarm in the house?"

"No, I don't believe so."

"Could someone have come in through that window, put some trace explosives in the basement, and then left?"

"That's not my area, Mr. Carpenter."

"Knowing how windows work is not your area? Have you lived a windowless existence? They are the glass things in walls; you can see through them."

Dylan objects that I'm badgering the witness and Judge Koenig sustains, again warning me to be careful. What a surprise.

"So you don't even know whether it's possible that someone came in through that window and left the trace explosives? Sergeant Jennings, I'm not asking for a definite answer as to whether it happened, nor a percentage of a quadrillion. I'm not even asking you as a forensics expert. I'm asking you as a thinking person if someone could possibly have come through that window."

Dylan again objects that I am badgering the witness, but this time Judge Koenig overrules him and instructs Jennings to answer.

"It is certainly possible that someone could have climbed in."

I give an exaggerated sigh, as if I don't know why this has to be like pulling teeth. "Thank you." With that tiny victory, I move on.

"Let's talk about Mr. Nash's car. The prosecution theory is that Mr. Nash was in the car, and the mayor's body was in the trunk, at least for the time it took to drive the three blocks to the park. You are aware of that theory?"

"Basically, yes."

"Who else was in the car?"

"What do you mean?"

"It was a six-word question; which part of it didn't you understand?"

Dylan objects again, and the judge warns me again. This is becoming a pattern.

"I don't know if anyone else was in the car," Jennings says.

"Do you know who was driving it?"

"I do not."

"Whose fingerprints were on the steering wheel?"

"There were none."

I had turned away briefly so I can turn back in a double take at this news. "Was Mr. Nash wearing gloves?"

"No."

"So a man so filled with drugs and alcohol as to render him almost or completely unconscious, who couldn't keep his car from going off into a ditch, had the wherewithal when the car landed to wipe the steering wheel clean?"

"I couldn't say."

"He was trapped in the car, unconscious, but he didn't want his fingerprints discovered because they would reveal that he had been in the car?"

"I can't say what happened; I wasn't there. I can only tell you what I found."

I nod. "And you have told us that, as well as what you didn't find. Thank you, Sergeant."

Dylan has saved what he considers his best for last.

He calls Linda Stokes, a vice president at AT&T, to testify about Bobby's cell phone.

She explains that phones have GPS signaling devices built into them, and that it can accurately be determined where a phone is or, retroactively when necessary, has been.

She says that she analyzed the records for Bobby's phone on the night in question, and Dylan puts up a map so that she can trace for the jury where it went.

As Dylan looks on happily, Stokes shows that the phone went to Mayor Oliva's house, then Eastside Park, then up the Palisades Interstate to where it went into the ditch.

Hours later, as she shows, the phone went with him to the hospital and stayed with him there.

This can obviously be devastating, and I can see the jury eating it up with a spoon. Bobby's phone was at the scene of the crime, the same phone was where the body was left, and Bobby never lost possession of the phone . . . what else is there to say?

Game, set, and match if I don't challenge it, and I'm reluctant to challenge it.

First of all, the facts are the facts, and I have no chance of changing them. Bobby's phone was there; what she is saying is accurate. No fancy cross-examination sleight of hand can change that.

More important, I am going to be using similar evidence in our case. So I don't want to question the science, because in a little while we are going to be relying on it.

I've got to be careful with this.

"Ms. Stokes, it is obvious that Mr. Nash's phone was in these places. Since that phone went with him to the hospital, it's a fair assumption that he was with the phone in that car. Who else was in the car?"

"I couldn't say."

"Was Mayor Oliva, alive or dead, in the car with him?"

"I couldn't say for sure."

"But he obviously might have been. Who else, if anyone, was in that car?"

"I don't know."

"But it's possible that there was another person, or maybe even two other people, in that car with Mr. Nash? Or with Mr. Nash and the mayor?"

"I really don't know."

"You really don't know if it's possible?"

"Oh . . . sorry. Yes, it's possible. I just can't tell one way or another from the data I have."

"I understand. Thank you. No further questions."

As Stokes leaves the stand, Dylan rises and says the words that I always simultaneously look forward to and dread hearing.

"The prosecution rests, Your Honor."

I am going to spend tonight getting ready to put on our case, but I do it differently from most lawyers I know.

I prepare the witness list, so I have to decide in what order I will call them. Eddie needs to know this so that he can have the witnesses alerted and ready on the right day. Judge Koenig, like every other judge in judicial history, does not look fondly on lawyers who do not have their witnesses in place.

I also go over in my mind what I want to ask the witnesses, though I only do so for those that will be called the next day. I never script out questions, but I do know what I need to get out of each one.

Preparing for prosecution witnesses is more difficult and more intense. In those cases I have to anticipate what they are going to say and come up with a way to counter those things in my cross-examination. With my defense witnesses, I already know what they are there to say; I just have to smoothly lead them to it.

The only exception is Richard Minchner, who I will not have a chance to interview in advance, and who will be unhappy to be there. I will probably have to ask Judge Koenig to let me treat him as a hostile witness, and the judge will likely grant that request.

There is a substantial likelihood that our defense will rise or fall on how successful I will be in carving up Minchner on the stand. I am certainly looking forward to trying.

I'm expecting our defense to last for three days, four at the most. Minchner will be the last to testify, unless we decide to have Bobby testify in his own defense.

I take the dogs for a fairly long walk, but we don't go into the park. Laurie asked me not to because she is concerned that Churasick or some other Jerry Conti employee will once again try to kill me.

I also think she made the request because it's easier for Marcus to keep track of me where there are streetlights, but then again, I think Marcus probably has X-ray vision. It's good that he does not wear a cape, because there are no longer phone booths where superheroes can change their clothes.

I spend the time thinking about and failing to answer what in my mind has become the key question. What does Conti have to gain by going through all of this to move into this area? There would be so many more lucrative places for him to go.

And for Joseph Russo, Jr., to go along with it, to make what must amount to a revenue-sharing deal with Conti, there must be enough new revenue to go around. Where the hell is it coming from?

After the walk I tuck Ricky into bed and head into the den to go over my witness list. I'm interrupted by a call from Sam, who says, "Minchner called Conti again."

"Interesting. How long did the call last?"

"Less than a minute. But he made it from his own cell phone this time; not from a company phone."

"He's getting nervous. Please tell Eddie to subpoena that phone record with the others. And tell him to add some other random days, so it doesn't appear that we already had the records and knew exactly what we would find."

"I'm on it."

After I hang up, I spend some more time on the witnesses and then head to the bedroom, where Laurie is watching the news. There is footage of Aaron Widener, candidate for governor, as he held a press conference earlier in the day.

Widener is, like every other politician, trying to profit from the reign of bombing terror that has hit Paterson. His technique is to criticize everyone in sight, and to vow that when he is running the state, all will be tranquil and safe. It's not exactly a gutsy political move to be the anti-bombing candidate.

"You ready?" Laurie says when I walk into the room.

Laurie in bed asking if I'm ready can have all different kinds of meanings, so I don't want to overreact.

"For what?"

"Tomorrow in court."

"Oh." I make no effort to conceal my disappointment.

"You need your rest, Andy."

"I'm actually well rested already. I'm afraid I'll be over-rested; there's nothing worse for a lawyer."

"Really? Why don't you do an hour on the treadmill?"

"Because I need my rest."

"Good night, Andy."

've arranged to meet with Bobby a half hour before the normal start of court today.

I'm waiting for him in the anteroom when he is brought in, and he looks worried, probably because this is the first time we've done this.

He takes a seat across the table from me. "Anything wrong?"

"You mean other than the fact that you're on trial for a double murder?"

He smiles. "Yes. Other than that."

"Nothing wrong. We just have to talk about the question of your testifying."

"Am I?"

"That's a decision that you and only you can make. In fact, if you decide not to, the judge will question you in open court to make sure you made the decision yourself, without any coercion from me."

"But what do you think?"

"I am almost always against it, but in this case I am even more strongly against it than usual."

"Why?"

"Because you have nothing to say that isn't self-serving

and unsupported by facts. You were unconscious and don't remember anything, but you're sure you couldn't have done it. You have no alibi, no explanation, you just don't remember."

"What about the explosion at Theresa Minardo's?"

"Again, you'll just say you didn't do it, without providing any proof. You can't prove a negative."

He thinks about this for a while, then, "You think we can win without me testifying?"

I nod. "I do. I also think we can lose. What I don't think is that you can help yourself on the stand. The risks dramatically outweigh the reward. But it's your call, and I will support it either way."

"I'm going with you."

That sums that up, so we spend the remaining time talking about how the trial has gone so far. He thinks we're doing better than we are, or I think we're doing worse than we are. One of us will be right.

"The prosecutor hates me," Bobby says. "I can feel it."

I shake my head. "'It's not personal, Sonny. It's strictly business.'"

"Sounds familiar . . . what's that line from?"

"*The Godfather.* It's the scene with Michael, Sonny, and Tom Hagen, the one when Michael decides to kill Sollozzo and the police captain."

Bobby nods. "Right. I was thinking it was Hyman Roth."

"No, Hyman Roth said, 'I didn't ask who gave the order, because it had nothing to do with business.' That was in *The Godfather Part II.*"

"You really love those movies, huh?"

I'm about to say that I do love them, but the bailiff comes in to tell us it's time to go into court.

I stand up and turn to Bobby. "Leave the table; take the cannoli."

Τ he defense calls Dr. Janine Dozier."

Dr. Janine Dozier has recently retired from a distinguished career treating drug addiction and related problems. She was even once on a presidential advisory council. So I spend some time letting her go through her impressive credentials; by the time she is done, the jury certainly will recognize her as an authority on the subject.

"Dr. Dozier, did you analyze the results of the blood test conducted on Mr. Nash at St. Joseph's Hospital?"

"Yes, I did."

"There has been testimony that there were high levels of fentanyl present in the blood, along with some alcohol."

"Yes. Actually, the alcohol was quite minimal."

"Would the alcohol level have been consistent with someone having two or three drinks seven or eight hours prior?"

She nods. "I would say so, yes."

"And the fentanyl level?"

"Extremely high. Depending on when it was ingested, it was at a level that could certainly have caused death."

"Let's talk about when it was taken; is it possible to determine that?"

"No, but we know it was at least three hours prior to

the blood being drawn, since it was that long since his car was discovered with him trapped inside."

"As you know, Mr. Nash was unconscious when found. He also had suffered a concussion. Would the fentanyl by itself have been sufficient to cause the unconsciousness?"

"Absolutely. Maintaining consciousness would have been extremely unlikely . . . almost impossible."

"Could he have operated a car with the blood levels reported?"

"Unless he took the drug shortly before the crash, before it would have completely taken effect, in my view there is simply no way he could have driven a car."

"And by 'shortly before,' how long do you mean?"

"Perhaps fifteen minutes."

"Can fentanyl be administered by injection?"

"Certainly."

"If administered in the dose we are talking about, is it possible that the person ingesting the drug could have no memory about either taking it voluntarily or having it forced on him?"

"Certainly memory loss in that situation is not just possible, but very probable."

Dylan starts his cross-examination with "Dr. Dozier, in your experience, I assume you have seen a significant number of deaths due to drug overdoses?"

"Unfortunately, yes."

"Some of those fentanyl?"

"Yes. Far too many."

"What about suicides? Have you seen deliberate overdoses that resulted in death?"

"Yes."

"Also, some of those were fentanyl?"

"Yes."

"Have you also seen murder suicides, where someone commits a homicide and then takes their own life by overdosing?"

"I have not personally been involved in such cases, but I certainly know they have happened."

"You have no idea how Mr. Nash came to get fentanyl in his system, do you?"

"I do not."

"And you don't know if he was suicidal, is that correct?"

"That is correct."

"Thank you. No further questions."

Dylan has done an outstanding job of negating the impact of our witness, by planting in the jurors' minds the idea that Bobby could have committed the murder and then tried to kill himself.

Such a scenario is consistent with his driving off the road, as well. It's an excellent and annoying piece of lawyering on Dylan's part.

Our next witness is Jacob Norris, a retired ATF agent with an expertise in explosives.

Norris has fashioned a new and lucrative career as an expert witness, testifying all over the country, but mostly on the East Coast. He has worked mostly for the defense side, mainly because the government has their own accessible experts in-house.

Norris does not come cheap, and the money is coming out of the overall defense budget, which also goes by the name of Andy Carpenter. But Norris is our only chance to explain away the trace explosives found in Bobby's basement.

Norris says that at my request he has examined all the evidence related to the explosion in Theresa Minardo's garage, and the trace evidence found in Bobby's basement.

"What was the explosive used to destroy the garage?"

"Cintron 421."

"Is it commercially available? Can I walk into a store and buy it?"

"You could not, no."

"Could I make it, if I had the expertise?"

"Yes. It is actually not that difficult, if you know what you're doing."

I ask him to explain what ingredients one would have to gather to make Cintron 421, and he lists five of them. One of the five is ammonium nitrate.

"So those materials would be brought in and then combined according to a formula to make the explosive?"

"In a manner of speaking, yes."

"Now, in Mr. Nash's basement, traces of Cintron 421 were found?"

"Yes."

"What about the other materials. Were traces of them found as well?"

"What do you mean?"

He knows exactly what I mean because he has gone over the testimony with Eddie. Norris is setting it up for me, which I appreciate. It's more evidence that this is not his first courtroom rodeo.

"Well, if there are traces of the finished product, the Cintron 421, shouldn't there also be traces of the individual materials that would have been left before the explosive was created?"

"There were no such traces of anything else."

"No ammonium nitrate, for example?"

"No."

"What about the tools necessary to make the explosive and the device that would carry it, were they found?"

"It's not in the inventory provided by the government."

"So based on what was found, there was no material and no tools, but, presto, an explosive was created? A hallelujah moment?"

He smiles. "That is what the evidence would indicate."

"Thank you."

Dylan frowns as if annoyed he has to deal with this nonsense.

"Dr. Norris, let me present a hypothetical for you. Assume for this purpose that the Cintron 421 was made elsewhere, not in Mr. Nash's basement. It was then brought into the basement and stored there until it was ready to be used. In this hypothetical, doesn't it make sense that there would be traces of the finished explosive, but not the individual materials?"

"Could be."

"And if it were made elsewhere, would there be any reason for the tools used in making it to be found in that basement?"

"I couldn't say."

"You don't have to. No further questions."

Dylan has sliced the witness up like a sturgeon. I had better up my game tomorrow.

Tomorrow is the day that we bring Churasick into the conversation. We're going to need to show that he and his boss, Conti, are people that the jury can logically think are the actual murderers.

Then the next day we bring Minchner onto the stand and into the picture and show his relationship with them.

We've got a shot, a decent shot, but it's going to have to go a hell of a lot better than our witnesses so far.

We flew Lieutenant Alvin Burgess in from Detroit two days ago and, ironically, put him up at the same Hilton where Richard Minchner and Theresa Minardo used to have their romantic liaisons.

He is third in the chain of command in the division of Detroit PD that deals with organized crime. In Detroit, that means he deals with Jerry Conti, with a side order of Drew Churasick thrown in.

That the department, even with some federal help, has not been able to nail Conti and Churasick made Burgess very willing to come here and do what he can to help.

I met with Burgess for about a half hour last night, as well as with another of our witnesses who works there. Eddie Dowd has done almost all the legwork in preparing our witnesses, but the fact that the first two have not gone particularly well is not his fault.

I've given him the marching orders and he's carried them out. What happens in the courtroom is on me.

When Burgess gets on the stand, I spend some time letting him tell the jury who he is and what he does within the Detroit PD. Once he has done that, I ask if he is familiar with Jerry Conti.

"Yes. In my opinion, and I certainly speak for the

department, Jerry Conti is the head of a crime family in the Detroit metropolitan area."

"Has he limited his operation to that area?"

"No, he has been expanding into other markets."

We talk about this a bit more, and then I ask if he is also familiar with Drew Churasick.

"Your Honor, I request a meeting in chambers." It's Dylan, clearly concerned about the direction this testimony is taking.

Judge Koenig agrees, so Eddie and I, as well as Dylan and two of his lawyers, head for the chambers. The court reporter establishes herself in there as well. Judge Koenig says, "Okay, we're on the record. Mr. Campbell?"

"Your Honor, Mr. Carpenter is conducting a fishing expedition. He is trying, without evidence, to implicate two men from Detroit in this case. It is a deliberate attempt at a smoke screen to confuse the jury, in the hopes of preventing a unanimous verdict."

Koenig turns to me. "Mr. Carpenter."

"First of all, let me state for the record that I want a unanimous verdict. It would be a terrible miscarriage of justice for one or two jurors to believe the nonsense that the prosecution has been peddling.

"Second, we will be introducing clear and convincing evidence tying Mr. Churasick to this case, today, in this courtroom. Mr. Campbell knows that fully well; he has received that evidence in discovery."

"Yesterday," Dylan says, the scorn evident in his voice.

I nod. "Hours after we received it. Unlike Mr. Campbell, we did not have to be compelled by the court to fulfill our discovery obligations promptly. I would have hoped that he would show more gratitude . . . maybe send flowers or at least a nice thank-you note."

"He waited until the last minute to subpoena it," Dylan says accurately. "He knew what he was going to find. We have not even had time to check its accuracy."

"Your Honor, we lived up to the letter of the law, one hundred percent. But if the court wishes to give the prosecution extra time so their four hundred lawyers can study the two pages of evidence we provided, we have no objection."

"Your Honor, that is an outrageous—"

Judge Koenig cuts Dylan off. "Here's what we will do. Mr. Carpenter, you can conduct your direct examination. And I caution you that I will be listening carefully to make sure that Mr. Campbell's description of this as a fishing expedition is not an accurate one.

"Once that is complete, Mr. Campbell can then conduct his cross-examination, or we can adjourn for the day and resume in the morning. It will be his choice."

I put on my most cheerful face. "Works for me, Your Honor."

We head back into court, and I resume questioning of Burgess, focusing most directly on Churasick. Burgess describes him as extremely dangerous and makes a pointed reference to his experience with explosives and ordnance in the army.

"If you know, was Drew Churasick ever listed as an employee by RMD Enterprises, whose chief executive is Richard Minchner?"

"Yes, he handled security for RMD."

"Do you have any information as to whether or not Drew Churasick has been in this area in the past two months?"

"Yes, there is TSA video of him at Newark Airport. He was using fake identification, which was not discovered at the time. His present whereabouts are unknown."

I introduce some documents as evidence and ask Burgess if I had previously given them to him and asked him to examine them. I also give copies to Dylan, to the court, and one to circulate among the jurors.

"Yes. I did so," Burgess says.

"The phone number on that page, which is redacted, is that a cell phone in the name of Drew Churasick?"

"Yes. And the address is one that is known to be his residence."

"These are GPS records showing where that phone was at eight fifteen P.M. on November twenty-fourth. Have you reviewed these?"

"Yes."

I use a map to have Burgess identify exactly where the phone was that night. He does so, and I point to a spot just adjacent to it. "Do you know who lived in this house at the time?"

"Yes. Theresa Minardo."

I pause for a beat to let the jury react and process this information, then I say, "Thank you, Lieutenant."

Judge Koenig asks Dylan if he wants to conduct his cross-examination now or resume tomorrow.

"We'll do it now, Your Honor."

"Very well, we'll take a fifteen-minute break and reconvene then."

I head to the bathroom, and when I come back, I'm surprised to see that Judge Koenig is already back at the bench. I can lose track of time, but I'm pretty sure I did not spend fifteen minutes in the bathroom.

Eddie Dowd and Bobby are still at the defense table, but Dylan walks over to talk to Judge Koenig. That's pretty unusual; ordinarily lawyers from both sides are present for every interaction with the judge.

I join them. "I was hoping to be invited to this party."

Judge Koenig says, "There has been another bombing, about four blocks from here. We have apparently not received a threat, but out of an abundance of caution we are going to adjourn for the day so the building can be searched."

I nod. "Good idea."

Court is not technically in session at the moment, so Judge Koenig sends the bailiff to clear out the people who are lingering in the gallery through the break. Police officers will also remove everyone from the building.

Dylan and I walk away from the bench together. "Do you know where the bomb went off?" I ask.

He shrugs. "I don't know any more than you do. See you tomorrow. Maybe." Then he stops. "A thank-you note and flowers?"

Then he smiles.

Laurie is watching television when I get home, and the coverage is obviously about the bombing.

Little information is being given out about it by the authorities, and the way they are carefully couching their comments makes me think that they know more than they want to reveal. All they are saying is that the target was a warehouse on Bergen Street.

More strange is that Mayor Womack has promised a press conference in two hours, with a leaked reveal to the press that he will be breaking big news. This seems to be different and somehow more significant than the bombings at the bus station and the American Legion Hall.

I call Vince to ask if he knows what is going on, since he's tied into the city hierarchy and must also have all of his reporters out on the street trying to run down the story. But he claims to be in the dark, so all we can do is wait.

About twenty minutes before the press conference, Pete Stanton calls me. "Because I'm a nice guy, I thought you should hear this from me."

His tone makes me anxious to hear what he has to say, so much so that I don't even take the time to insult him.

He continues, "There were two victims in today's bombing, both deceased."

"Who are they?"

"Drew Churasick and Richard Minchner."

Kaboom.

"Do you know who did it?"

"Looks like they did," Pete says.

"What the hell does that mean?"

"Watch Womack's press conference. I don't want to get ahead of it, and there might be new information that I don't know. What I'm telling you is as of a half hour ago, and the Feds are all over what used to be that warehouse trying to figure it all out."

I can't get any more information out of Pete, so I tell Laurie about the conversation and then all we can do is wait impatiently for the press conference.

My mind hasn't even fully processed this news, in that I can't yet figure out what effect it will have on the case. Maybe Womack will say something that will help in that regard.

I take the dogs for a quick walk; I want to be back in time to hear what Womack has to say. Sebastian, unfortunately, does not share my desire to hurry things, and by the time I get back, Womack is just about to speak.

He is standing at a podium in the pressroom at City Hall. He is alone; no federal officers, no local cops, and certainly no Commissioner Bauer. If there is a spotlight, Womack seems not inclined to share it.

"As you know, another bomb was detonated in downtown Paterson, this one in a warehouse on Bergen Street," Womack says. "There were two fatalities; the victims have been identified as Richard Minchner, a local businessman, and Drew Churasick, of Detroit.

"I cannot get too far into the details of exactly what transpired, but this does not appear to have been an intentional attack. We are in the early stages of the investigation, but there is evidence that this is where the explosive devices were being manufactured.

"The deceased, Mr. Minchner and Mr. Churasick, have been persons of interest in the other bombing incidents, which I consider acts of terrorism. We had been closing in on them, and an arrest was imminent. I believe they were aware of that fact. Whether it was a factor in today's incident, I cannot be sure yet.

"I would like to thank the FBI, ATF, and New Jersey State Police for their remarkable investigative work. They will continue their work until we know all the facts. We will then report them to you in the most transparent way possible.

"Thank for your attention."

With that Womack walks off, as the reporters futilely shout out questions.

"He hung Bauer out to dry again by not mentioning him or the Paterson PD," Laurie says.

I nod. "Politics is a twenty-four-seven game."

"Do you think the detonation was accidental? Or do you think they were murdered?"

I think about that for a few seconds. "With the disclaimer that I have no idea what is going on, I think they were murdered."

"Why?"

"A couple of reasons, the main one being Minchner's presence. He would have no reason to be part of the bomb-making process; he tried to keep clean and above the fray.

I don't think he would have put himself in that position voluntarily. I don't see him hanging out in a warehouse working the explosive conveyer belt."

"And the other reason?"

"This has the feel of loose ends being cleaned up. As if Conti got what he wanted, whatever the hell that is. But now he wants to eliminate anybody who knows about it."

She nods. "I think you're right. But it raises another disturbing issue. Conti has brought someone in who was able to handle Churasick. At least in Churasick's case we knew who we were looking for and watching out for; now we have no idea."

"That's true and it's depressing. Maybe it's the other guy who flew in with Churasick, the one who didn't show up at our house that night."

"What does this do for Bobby's situation?"

"That's another thing I don't know; I have to think it through. But one thing is definite."

"What's that?"

"James Pritchett was right when he said that Richard Minchner wouldn't obey the subpoena. He has successfully avoided testifying."

Judge Koenig doesn't wait for Dylan or me to ask for a meeting in chambers.

He has the bailiffs bring us back there as soon as we show up for court. The news from yesterday obviously has an effect on our case, and he wants to make sure he controls as much of it as he can.

"Well, gentlemen, we have things to talk about. The real world seems to have intruded on our trial."

I let Dylan speak first, mainly because I like to play defense more than offense. It's just a personality thing; for the same reason I prefer doing cross-examinations to direct ones.

"Your Honor, the events of yesterday have no business becoming part of this trial," Dylan says. "Mr. Carpenter has injected outside factors that do not bear on the jury's job; they are here to determine and judge the actions of the defendant.

"Churasick and Minchner, as I stated yesterday, are not relevant to this case. They may well have been bad guys, and that's possibly why they died. We don't know that yet; an investigation will determine it. But nothing that happened to them has anything to do with whether or not Bobby Nash murdered Alex Oliva and Theresa Minardo. That evidence stands separate and alone and remains compelling."

I shake my head. "Your Honor, with all due respect to Mr. Campbell, the only way I can make sense of his position is in the context of a desperate effort to save his case."

"Your Honor . . . ," Dylan says, obviously angry. For some reason he doesn't finish his sentence, though I give him a couple of seconds to do it, and Judge Koenig does not respond.

So I continue, "We already introduced evidence yesterday tying Mr. Churasick to this case. We were and are preparing to do the same with Mr. Minchner; in fact, he was going to be called as a witness. Further, Mr. Campbell alleged that the motive for Mr. Nash's killing spree was a grudge caused by an event in which Mr. Minchner was a key player.

"But this case involves a bombing murder. Now two people involved in the trial themselves die in a bombing, and we are supposed to dismiss it as irrelevant and not fit for the jury to hear? That would not be fair on any planet I am familiar with."

Dylan shakes his head. "Your Honor, here on earth, this information is far more prejudicial than probative. There is not a shred of evidence, as far as I know, that ties the most recent bombing to this case. All this jury should be concerned about and weighing is the evidence against Bobby Nash."

I nod. "And they should have all the facts to do so. Your Honor, I need to go on record here. If this information is not allowed in, I will ask the court for a mistrial. If it is not granted, I would request that Your Honor grant a continuance so that I can file an appeal. Anything less would be unfair to my client, and my not making those requests would represent ineffective counsel."

My saying this is a risk. First of all, it's extremely rare for an appeal to move forward during a criminal trial. Civil yes, criminal no, but it could conceivably happen, and my bringing it up is my effort to show how serious this situation is.

But more important, Judge Koenig could angrily interpret it as a threat, mainly because it was a threat. Not only that, but it was an empty one, because I don't want a mistrial, and I would want to preserve my right to appeal the decision for after the trial should we lose.

Fortunately, Koenig does not seem angry at all. "I think an appeal would be justified. I don't agree that the information is more prejudicial than probative, Mr. Campbell. I think what happened represents facts, which the triers of fact can weigh in their deliberations.

"I also will offer new instructions to the jury. As you know, up to this point I have instructed them to avoid media coverage of this case. I will extend that embargo to coverage of the bombings . . . all the bombings."

"That ship has sailed," Dylan says. "It has been on television twenty-four seven, and on the front page of every newspaper, including the New York papers. It has dominated the media."

Judge Koenig nods. "To some degree it has, but the court can only do what the court can do."

That's sort of hard to argue with.

We head back into court, and I have ten minutes to meet with Lieutenant Burgess to update him before he continues his testimony. Dylan was about to cross-examine him when we adjourned yesterday.

I tell Burgess that he can mention the bombings yesterday. He was worried that to do so might prompt a mistrial, but I assure him that the judge has okayed it.

I go back into court to brief Bobby on what is going on. His access to news in the jail is limited.

"Eddie's been telling me about it," he says. "What the hell does it mean for us? Will it help?"

"Bobby, we're in uncharted territory."

While Dylan can't restrict the information the jury will hear, he can control the manner in which they hear it.

I wish I hadn't finished my direct examination of Lieutenant Burgess; then I would have been able to be in charge. Instead Dylan has the floor, and he tackles the situation head-on.

"Lieutenant Burgess, yesterday you were talking about a Detroit resident named Drew Churasick. Was he killed in yesterday's bombing on Bergen Street?"

"Yes."

"Was another victim one Richard Minchner?"

"Yes."

"Do you have any information which would lead you to believe that the incident yesterday had anything to do with this case?"

"I have no information about it at all. It's not my case. That is not my case; nor is this one."

"So that's a no?"

"I do not have any knowledge of a connection between that incident and this case."

"Thank you. Now yesterday you referred to telephone

records of a phone in Mr. Churasick's name. That phone was on a street near Theresa Minardo's house, correct?"

"Behind her house, yes."

"Do you know if Mr. Churasick was there? Could someone else have been carrying his phone?"

"I only know about the phone."

Dylan nods as if now we're getting somewhere. "Do you know what whoever had the phone was doing there?"

"No."

"Is there anything illegal about being on a street near Theresa Minardo's house?"

"Depends on what they are doing."

"And you just said you don't know what they were doing. I'm asking if their presence there was inherently illegal."

"No."

"Thank you."

My next witness is Carl McKenzie, the limo driver who drove Theresa Minardo to and from the hotel that night. He is clearly nervous, though he has no reason to be. He's purely a fact witness and won't be on the stand long.

I let him identify himself as an employee of Elite Limousines and then ask, "On the night of November twenty-fourth, did you pick up Theresa Minardo at her house at around six thirty?"

"I did."

"Where did you take her?"

"To the Hilton Hotel in the Meadowlands."

"Did you then pick her up later that night at around eleven thirty and bring her back home?"

"Yes."

"Do you know what she was doing there?"

"Based on a phone conversation she had in the car, I believe she was meeting a man. It was a sedan, so I couldn't help but hear the call. I try not to."

"I understand. Did she mention during the call what room she was going to?"

"Yes. Nine fourteen. I remembered that because my birthday is September fourteenth. That's nine fourteen."

I guess he was worried that the jury would not pick up on that. "Did you drive Ms. Minardo to that hotel on a regular basis?"

"I'm not sure I would call it regular, but I probably took her there seven or eight times in the last couple of years."

"Were you the only driver who did so?"

"Oh, no."

Dylan starts his cross by asking, "Mr. McKenzie, was there anything unusual about that night?"

"What do you mean?"

"If you hadn't been interviewed and called to testify for this case, would that night have been more memorable than any other?"

"I guess not; just another work night."

"Do you know who Ms. Minardo was meeting at the hotel?"

"No."

"Do you know why she was meeting him?"

"I can guess."

This draws laughter from some in the gallery, which Dylan cuts short by saying, "We don't do guesswork here. Do you know the answer?"

"No."

"Thank you. No further questions."

My last witness for the day is Katie Corneau, Theresa Minardo's friend and coworker on the long-defunct committee working to elect Alex Oliva to the governorship of New Jersey.

She had not mentioned to me that Theresa was having an affair with Richard Minchner, but had willingly said so to Laurie. Katie now tells the entire world through her testimony; I am apparently the only person she wouldn't share it with.

Dylan shrugs it off and barely cross-examines her, acting as if it is unimportant.

It will become more important tomorrow.

Tomorrow is Richard Minchner day, may he rest in peace.

Today is going to be a day of inference. We're going to imply shady things about Richard Minchner, without giving any proof of actual shadiness.

My first witness is Henry Garcia, a desk clerk at the Hilton Hotel in the Meadowlands. He testifies that both Richard Minchner and Theresa Minardo visited the hotel on occasion, arriving separately but staying in the same room.

He also confirms that the reservations for the room were always made in Minchner's company's name, and that the room service orders were always the same . . . two shrimp cocktails, chocolate-covered strawberries, sorbet, and a bottle of champagne.

Those two crazy kids were not really into full, well-balanced meals.

Dylan has only a couple of perfunctory questions for Garcia. There is nothing new here. Everybody, jury included, already knows that Minchner and Theresa were having an affair; Katie Corneau confirmed that. And the limo driver has previously made it clear that their destination of choice was the Hilton.

Next up is one of the witnesses that Dylan had called, Linda Stokes of AT&T. Dylan had gotten her to place

Bobby's cell phone at Alex Oliva's house and Eastside Park, testimony that remains among the most damaging to Bobby.

"Ms. Stokes, did you examine all of Mr. Nash's phone GPS records, at my request?"

"I did. I had also already done it at Mr. Campbell's direction."

I smile. "Sorry we are doubling your workload."

She returns the smile. "Happy to help."

"In all the records you examined, was Mr. Nash's phone ever in the vicinity of Theresa Minardo's house?"

"It was not."

"Are you sure?"

"Yes."

"Now, did I ask you to examine the phone records for Richard Minchner?"

"Yes. His home, his cell, and his office."

"And did I ask you to look for specific calls he might have made?"

She nods. "Yes, I was asked to look for calls to or from Mr. James Conti in Detroit."

"Did you find any?"

"I did not find any calls to any of those numbers initiated by Mr. Conti, but there were three calls made from those numbers to him. Two were from Richard Minchner's office phone, and the most recent from his cell phone."

"Thank you."

Dylan asks, "Ms. Stokes, could Mr. Nash have been at Theresa Minardo's house without carrying his phone?"

"I assume so."

"Would you know it from his records if he was?"

"No, sir."

"Thank you."

During lunch Eddie and I sit with Lieutenant Pierce, not to go over his testimony or script what he is going to say, but just to let him know what areas I want to cover.

He has refused to meet with Eddie prior to this, probably because he hates defense lawyers in general, and me in particular. I was pretty rough on him during cross-examination when he testified for the prosecution.

After we go over things, I can tell that he's still pissed. "I hope you're not upset about my cross-examination."

"You can hope."

"We're all here to see that justice is done" is my next try at reconciliation.

"Yeah, right."

This could be a problem.

Lieutenant Pierce, this is a murder trial, but I'd like to start by talking to you about a couple of attempted murders."

He doesn't respond; I was looking for an "Okay" or a "Fine." This could be a painful direct examination. I want to avoid asking Judge Koenig to let me treat Pierce as a hostile witness; it could annoy Pierce and become a self-fulfilling prophecy.

I continue, "Are you familiar with an incident that happened to the defendant at St. Joseph's Hospital while he was there recovering from injuries suffered in the car accident?"

"Yes."

"Can you relate it for the jury, please?"

"He was poisoned and nearly died."

"Who poisoned him?"

"That has not been determined yet. We do know that the poison was put into his food, but we do not know how that was accomplished."

"So the investigation is ongoing?"

"Yes."

"Next, was there an incident at my house that you are familiar with?"

"Yes. Two men attempted to abduct you at gunpoint."

"Was this at night?"

"Yes."

"What was the result of their attempt?"

"One of the men was killed and the other badly injured. Two of your investigators were on the scene and prevented them from succeeding in that attempt."

Pierce gives the names of the two men, and I ask if he has checked into their background.

"Yes. They were from Detroit. Both had police records."

"Were they associates of anyone that has been mentioned in this trial?"

"Yes. Drew Churasick."

"The same Drew Churasick who was killed along with Richard Minchner in the recent explosion?"

"Yes."

"So just to recap, and not including the attempt on Mr. Nash's life, in recent days there have been two deaths of people connected to this trial, and an attempt on the life of one of the lawyers, in this case me. Is that an accurate summary?"

"Yes."

"Has Mr. Nash been in custody while all this has been going on?"

"Yes, he has."

"Is he a suspect in the deaths of Mr. Churasick or Mr. Minchner?"

"No."

"Or the attempted abduction of yours truly?"

"No."

"Thank you." I turn to Dylan. "Your witness."

Pierce has done fine; he's masked his dislike for me and answered the questions directly, if not eloquently.

"Lieutenant, do you have any idea who is responsible for the bombing that killed Mr. Churasick and Mr. Minchner?"

"No, I don't. But I am not working that case."

"To your knowledge, is there still consideration given to the possibility that it was an accident?"

"I only know that from media reports."

"Let's talk about Mr. Churasick. Do you know anything that connects him to Mayor Alex Oliva?"

"I do not."

"You arrested Mr. Nash for the murder of Mr. Oliva, did you not?"

"I did."

"Sitting here today, with the knowledge of all the things that you testified about, do you think you did the right thing in making that arrest?"

"I do."

"Thank you."

I stand and say, "Your Honor, the defense rests."

Various things have different standards of success. Take sports as an excellent example.

In baseball, if a batter gets three hits in every ten tries, he's an all-star. An NFL quarterback is doing well if he completes 65 percent of his passes, and if you are shooting three-pointers in the NBA, then 40 percent is extraordinary.

In real life, some things require 100 percent perfect outcomes. Parachutes come to mind. As does representing defendants against multiple murder charges. Fifty percent, meaning one conviction and one acquittal, is a disaster. Serving forty years in jail for one murder isn't all that different from serving forty years in jail for two murders, although the latter might offer higher status among certain fellow inmates.

Unfortunately, a split decision is a definite possibility here. I think we have mounted a much better defense to the Minardo murder than the Oliva one.

We have put Churasick at Theresa's house, which is crucial. We have exposed her affair with Minchner, and that he seems to have drawn her away from her house that night when Churasick showed up. And we have made the connection between Churasick and Minchner, an easy one to make since they died together.

The only thing they have to tie Bobby to her murder is the trace explosives and the alleged grudge he had against her. I think we were fairly effective in countering those aspects, but time will tell.

We've done less to shift blame from Bobby in the Oliva killing. We scored major points on the drug evidence, and I think we scored on the lack of blood on his clothing and the illogic of bringing the body three blocks to Eastside Park.

But Dylan has accomplished a lot, and I have my doubts that we were able to refute enough of it.

I call Pete and ask him if the investigators have concluded whether the bomb that killed Churasick and Minchner went off accidentally or was intentionally detonated by someone.

"What am I, your information service?"

Pete is always pleasant and charming. "Believe me, I wish there was someone competent I could call, but you're all I've got for now."

He pauses for a moment, probably trying to think of a snappy comeback, but comes up blank. "I'm not involved in the investigation; the department has been frozen out so Mayor Womack can play with the big boys and make Commissioner Bauer look bad."

"You know some of those big boys. What are they saying?"

"That they may never know for certain, but they don't believe it was an accident."

"Why won't they know for certain?"

"Because a bomb went off, okay? It doesn't exactly leave fingerprints. How would anyone know if it went off accidentally or not?"

"But you said they don't think it was an accident."

"Right. Because Churasick was a pro, for one thing. Pros don't screw up like that. And because Minchner was there. Minchner was not in the violence business; the most dangerous thing he did was drink really hot coffee."

Both of those were points I made to Laurie. "Makes sense."

"Wonderful; now I feel validated," Pete says. "How's your trial going?"

"Could go either way."

"My guy Pierce is not your biggest fan. He didn't like the way you treated him in cross."

"I'll send him flowers."

I get off with Pete and think about what he said. If the bomb that killed Churasick and Minchner went off accidentally, then no conclusions are to be drawn from it.

But if Pete is right, and I think he is, then Conti has sent someone else in to eliminate those two. It could be the other guy who flew in with Churasick and the guys at my house. He hasn't shown up on our radar yet, but he might have killed Churasick and Minchner and is therefore the last one standing.

Conti must have accomplished his goal, and he's cleaning up. It's a sign of his ruthlessness that two people who did his bidding and dirty work are considered loose ends, but it seems to me that's what happened.

Hovering over all of this in my mind is what the hell

Conti wanted in the first place. Why is he moving into this area, and why did he have to go through all this to do it? Why not just make a deal with Russo and set up shop?

Why did Alex Oliva, Theresa Minardo, Churasick, and Minchner have to die?

Mr. Carpenter, this is James Pritchett. Can we talk?"
He's called me on my cell phone just thirty seconds after I get in my car. It surprises me because I just saw him as we were both leaving the courthouse, and he didn't say a word. Now he wants to talk?

"Aren't we talking now?"

"I meant in person. Somewhere we wouldn't be seen."

I quickly toss the possibilities around in my head. I certainly don't fully trust this guy, so I don't want him to come to my house. My mind is drawn again to a quote from the great Michael Corleone: "In my home! In my bedroom where my wife sleeps! Where my children come and play with their toys."

But instead of going full *Godfather* on Pritchett, I just say, "Meet me at my office at eight o'clock. It's on Van Houten Street near—"

"I know where it is. I'll see you there at eight. But just you and me, please."

When I get home, I tell Laurie about the phone call. "There is no way you will be there alone with this guy."

"Laurie, I've met him. I literally could beat him up, and I don't say that about many people above the age of eight."

"What if he has a weapon? Can you handle that? I'm talking about a weapon more dangerous and substantial than biting sarcasm."

I ignore that, which I always do when she makes a good point. "The last time I talked to him, he seemed like he wanted to turn on Minchner. Maybe the fact that Minchner is dead has given him the courage to actually do it."

"Good for him. Let him do it in your conference room, with Marcus in your office listening along with you. And with Corey and me waiting outside, just in case."

"Who am I meeting with, a wimpy vice president, or the Russian army?"

"This is not negotiable, Andy. I am not looking for your okay."

She may not be looking for my okay, but I am not going to let her push me around. I'm going to give it to her anyway: "Okay."

That'll teach her.

I call Sam because I don't want Marcus to be the only surprise for Pritchett as a result of our meeting. I tell him what I want and he says what he always says: "You got it."

I head down to the office early, first dropping Ricky off at Will Rubenstein's house. Ricky has been staying there a lot; I think Will's parents are going to start charging us rent. Laurie and Corey will join me at the office later and are working out their own transportation.

I run today's court session through my mind, which I often do, trying to think of potential openings or pitfalls that the testimony presented. Something that was said is bugging me, sitting in the dark recesses of my mind, but I can't quite think of what it was.

Usually when that happens it turns out to be something important, or something completely meaningless . . . I never know until I think of what it was. It's frustrating; it's not like trying to place an actor, or the lyrics of a song. This is not something I can google.

I arrive at the office suite at seven thirty and open the locked outer door. Sitting inside on a chair is Marcus. I have no idea how he got in here; he doesn't have a key. On the other hand, he's Marcus. Maybe he beamed himself in.

"Marcus."

"Yuhh," he says.

The weird thing is that Marcus is highly intelligent, well-read, and even a lover of classical music. He just chooses not to communicate with other humans, with the exception of Laurie.

Marcus goes into my private office, leaving the door slightly ajar. Even though I am truly not worried or afraid of James Pritchett, it's comforting having Marcus here.

Pritchett arrives at eight o'clock on the nose. I let him in through the door that leads to the conference room. He looks around. "This is your office?"

"It's actually the conference room. It's more elegant than my office."

"You're a big-time lawyer . . . this place is a shithole."

"I'm glad my decorator isn't around to hear you say that."

He looks at a chair with an expression that says he'd like to set fire to it, but he sits in it instead.

I sit in a chair across from him. "The floor is yours."

He nods. "I just have to preface this by saying I will never say publicly what I am saying to you tonight. I would be afraid of the repercussions. I'm sure I could have

legal jeopardy for not coming forward sooner, but the nonlegal jeopardy might be more severe."

"Okay."

"Richard Minchner was involved in a business relationship with Drew Churasick; I believed . . . I believe . . . they killed Theresa Minardo."

"Why?"

"I'm not sure; understand I was not part of any of these discussions . . . but . . . I think they also killed Alex Oliva. I think that Theresa may have been killed to make the case against your client even stronger."

That confirms something I have thought since the beginning, but I don't say so. "What reason would they have for killing Oliva?"

"It's all about Aaron Widener. He's running for governor."

"I know Widener."

"They own him; Widener is in their pocket."

"Who is 'they'?"

"Churasick and Minchner; I don't know who else was involved."

"Jerry Conti ring a bell?"

"I have no firsthand knowledge of that—really, I don't."

"What about Joseph Russo?"

Pritchett laughs at the mention of the name. "Junior? This much I do know: whoever is behind this will tolerate him for a little while and then send him on his way. Whether he wants to go or not."

"Russo might have a different point of view on that."

"Junior will be in over his head. That's for sure."

"What are they hoping to get from Widener?"

"I don't know that either. I believe it might involve drugs."

"So who killed Churasick and Minchner?"

"As far as I know, it was an accident. They were meeting to plan their next steps. I can't imagine who would have wanted to kill them."

"Why were all these bombings happening?"

"I'm sorry to be difficult, but I can't be sure of that either. At one point they were planning those things to make Oliva look bad, but I know they didn't like Womack, the acting mayor. Maybe they wanted to hurt him."

"Didn't work out; Womack comes out of this looking like the scourge of terrorists."

"Doesn't matter anymore."

"What about the original story Bobby ran? The one about Minchner and the illegal contributions?"

"It was a stupid idea that Minchner and Theresa had to make Oliva look bad. Then it all blew up in their faces, and they backed off. They didn't think it through." Pritchett pauses and takes a deep breath. "Then they found another way to deal with Oliva."

I'm wondering what Pritchett's agenda is here; he's certainly not coming forward out of a sudden thirst to see justice prevail. All I can do right now is ask him, although it is not likely to get me the real answer. "Why are you telling me all this?"

"Who else am I going to tell? If the police knew I was aware of this stuff, I could go away for a while. And I really don't want your client to spend the rest of his life in jail."

"I could subpoena you to testify to this. I can ask the judge to reopen the defense case and put you on the stand."

"You can get me to court, but I won't say what you'd want to hear. This is as far as it goes; I've gotten it off my chest and now it's up to you."

"So now your conscience is clear."

Pritchett smiles sadly. "Clearer . . . not clear. But it's the best I can do right now. I hope it helps."

We've been through a lot together," Dylan says, smiling, as he starts his closing statement.

"As murder trials go, this one has not lasted particularly long, but I'll bet it seemed a lot longer to you. That's because every day, every hour, every witness statement, has been packed with tension. It's the nature of the beast, because there is so much at stake.

"Two people are dead, cut down in the prime of life. One was the mayor, and one had a more so-called regular job, but they are equal in importance, both in the eyes of the law, in my eyes, and I'm sure in your eyes as well.

"If Robert Nash took the lives of these people, he deserves to go to prison. If he didn't, he deserves to go free. It's as simple as that. And as I told you in my opening statement, you have to make that decision, one way or the other. It's at least as important as any you will ever make.

"But the fact that the decision is momentous doesn't mean it's difficult. I told you that also. I told you that we would give you enough evidence, incontrovertible evidence, to demonstrate beyond a reasonable doubt, that Robert Nash, coldly and with premeditation, committed the acts of which he stands accused.

"Mr. Nash had an intense grudge against both Mayor

Oliva and Theresa Minardo. He made no secret of it; he told anyone who'd listen. He thought they destroyed his career, despite the fact that he and no one else ran that false story.

"We showed you that he was at the scene of Mr. Oliva's killing, and also where the body was left. We proved that the victim's blood was in the trunk of his car. We demonstrated conclusively that the explosive used to kill Ms. Minardo was in his basement. What was it doing there? Is there an innocent explanation? Is there Cintron 421 in your basement? I don't think so. I certainly hope not.

"There are things we don't know and probably never will. For example, the drugs that Mr. Nash used that night. Did he use them to fortify himself to commit the murder? Or was he trying to commit suicide? Is that also why he crashed his car?

"But the bottom line is that for your purposes, it doesn't matter. You just have to judge his actions as they relate to the two innocent victims in this case.

"Mr. Carpenter is an excellent lawyer. He spun a mesmerizing tale about evil criminals from Detroit coming here to murder and blame Mr. Nash. But did you ask yourself why they did that? What brought them to Paterson, New Jersey? Mr. Carpenter never got around to that.

"It defies logic, but it certainly was entertaining.

"I believe that a fair look at the evidence will lead you to the inescapable conclusion that Robert Nash, beyond a reasonable doubt, took the lives of Alex Oliva and Theresa Minardo.

"I ask that you do your job, that you follow Judge Koenig's instructions, and come up with a fair and just verdict. I know you will."

Mr. Campbell just told you, and Judge Koenig will tell you, and I am telling you . . . to convict Robert Nash of these crimes you must be certain of his guilt beyond a reasonable doubt."

I walk slowly around the front of the courtroom, near the jury box, as I talk. I do not have a prepared speech; I want this to feel like a conversation I am having with the jury.

"I will go over the evidence with you, but since I've started off with reasonable doubt, let's start by focusing for the moment on one witness's testimony.

"Nancy Oliva is the widow of Alex Oliva. No one on this planet wants her husband's killer to be brought to justice more than she does. She came into this court and told you that she received two phone calls from a man claiming to be Mr. Nash, threatening her husband. One call came on the day he died, and one on the day before.

"She told you that she came to realize that it was not Mr. Nash who made the calls, and she explained that she is literally an expert in the field of voice detection. She has her master's in it . . . she made a career of it. And she said it was not Mr. Nash."

"Isn't it reasonable to assume that she might be right?

Lieutenant Pierce thought it was; he said so right on the stand. And what does it mean if she's right? Well, for one thing, it means that someone out there was pretending to be Mr. Nash to make it look like he was a threat to Alex Oliva.

"That person, it is also reasonable to assume, was framing Mr. Nash before the murder was even committed. Knowing that such a person is out there, I would submit, literally defines reasonable doubt.

"And the rest of the state's case is clearly weak in many areas, and nonsensical in others. I believe we have demonstrated that.

"Why would the killer have shot Mr. Oliva, loaded his body in the trunk of the car, and dropped it three blocks away? How about so there would be blood evidence in Mr. Nash's car? And how did someone Mr. Nash's size manage to lift a blood-soaked body, much larger than he is, into the car without getting blood on him?

"Why would he wipe his fingerprints from a car he was trapped in? Mr. Campbell suggests a possible suicide attempt. So he wiped his fingerprints so the police would think it was a different dead body they were looking at in the car?

"Why didn't the police stop to think that maybe someone went into Mr. Nash's house through that open window and conveniently left the trace explosives there, while he was in the hospital?"

"The list of reasonable questions goes on and on. And I haven't even gotten into Mr. Churasick, who was at Ms. Minardo's house, or Mr. Minchner, who placed three calls to a crime boss who employed Mr. Churasick.

"And what about the attempts on my life and Mr. Nash's life? Or the murders of Churasick and Minchner? Homicides and attempted homicides were popping up all over, while Mr. Nash had a perfect alibi . . . he was in jail.

"I ask you to do one thing: consider all of this, and use your common sense to guide you. Thank you."

I head back to the defense table; my legs feel like they are made of concrete. This is the worst feeling of all, and I experience it in every case.

It's over. It's done. There is no longer anything I can do; it is totally out of my hands.

It is a lack of control and fear that I did not do enough that literally leaves me nauseous.

This is why I have been trying to retire.

When this is officially over, when the jury has come back, if I have any regrets, they will definitely involve James Pritchett. I only wish I could have taken the information he belatedly provided and made some use of it.

For the most part, he basically confirmed everything we suspected and were trying to get the jury to understand, but his absolute refusal to testify made him useless to me.

The one new piece of information, and it was a blockbuster, is that Aaron Widener, the favorite for governor in November, was in the pocket of Minchner. Since Minchner had taken up residence in Jerry Conti's pocket, that means the governor of New Jersey might well be doing the bidding of organized crime.

Widener had gotten uptight and angry when I pressed him on his relationship with Minchner. I thought it might have been a concern about campaign contributions, but based on what Pritchett told me, it was a hell of a lot more than that.

It's not going to help Bobby Nash, but one thing is for sure: I am going to spend the time between now and November exposing Widener's complicity.

For now I just have to live with this awful feeling that I get when the jury is about to deliberate. And this time it's going to last even longer, because it's Saturday and Judge Koenig won't be charging the jury until Monday, when they will start their deliberations. It is literally painful, and I have to try to get my mind to think about other things.

But right now all I can focus on is how much I hate Vince Sanders for getting me into this in the first place.

S peaking of Vince Sanders, he shows up at our door just a few minutes after I get back from the morning walk with the dogs. He has Duchess with him, of course.

A boy and his dog.

"Hey, we're heading to the park. You want to come? She's got a whole bunch of new tricks I can show you." He turns and says in a baby voice, "Don't you, little girl?"

"Vince, you're making me nauseous. And as appealing as the park sounds, I'm just going to stay home, watch some college basketball, and pound my head against the wall."

"You did a great job in the trial."

"The jury will have something to say about that."

"Well, I really want to thank you, no matter how it comes out. I owe you one."

"That's comforting."

"You in a bad mood?" he asks.

"What tipped you off?"

"How come? Just nervous?"

"I am in a bad mood because I know that Bobby is innocent, and I am afraid he is going to go to jail for the rest of his life."

"I'm glad you've come to believe in him."

"I don't just believe in him. I know he's innocent for a fact."

"How?"

"James Pritchett came to see me. He's Minchner's right-hand guy."

Vince nods. "I know who he is. What did he have to say?"

I'm about to relate the conversation when I realize there are no secrets anymore. "You can listen to it yourself; I had Sam secretly tape the conversation. He transferred it to my phone."

I grab my phone and hit the buttons that Sam told me to hit. Amazingly, it works, and Pritchett's voice fills the room.

Vince is silent as we listen to Pritchett tell me about Churasick and Minchner, and how they killed Alex Oliva and Theresa Minardo. Vince looks particularly interested when Pritchett mentions Joseph Russo, Jr., and talks about how they owned Widener.

When the recording is over, Vince says, "Wow . . . you couldn't use that?"

"No. First of all, I got it after the defense case was over. But he also was careful to couch everything in 'I think' or 'I believe' or 'I'm not sure, but.' The way he presents it, it's all hearsay—stuff he overheard. If we lose, I'll try and include it in an appeal, but it's not going to carry the day."

"He sounded pretty sure about the Widener part. I never would have guessed that. Widener is an asshole, but I always thought he was a pretty honest one . . . relatively speaking."

"And are you ready for this? Oliva had decided not to

run for governor; he said he was needed in Paterson. His wife told me."

"So why did they kill him?"

"Because he hadn't announced it. He had only told a few city officials; he hadn't even told his staff, and . . ."

I stop talking because I've started thinking. I find it difficult to do both at the same time.

"He hadn't even told his staff, and what?" Vince asks.

"Vince, you're a genius. You're even smarter than Duchess."

"I don't know why you are saying that, but nobody is smarter than Duchess."

"Vince, take your brilliant dog to the park. I have some thinking and planning to do."

want to speak to Joseph Russo. This is Andy Carpenter." I tried to talk in a tone that didn't reflect my nervousness, but I don't think I pulled it off.

"He know you?

"Yes. I'm a lawyer."

"A lawyer?" He said it with slightly less respect than he might have said, *A locust?*

"Yes."

"Hold on."

I held on for about five extremely long minutes. I was trying to decide whether to hang up when he came back. "He'll call you back."

"When?"

"When he calls you back."

"Tell him it's really important. I have information for him that he will want to know."

Click.

Either the guy didn't deliver the message, or Joseph Russo, Jr., wasn't impressed by it, because he didn't call me back until Sunday night, thirty-six hours after I made the call.

And he didn't actually call me back at all; instead it was

the same guy who answered the phone when I had called. He hadn't progressed much as a conversationalist.

"Tomorrow night at nine o'clock. Giarusso's."

Giarusso's is a restaurant in the Riverside section of Paterson, not far from Russo's house. The entire area qualifies as his home base. Of course, when I meet with the man they call Junior, he doesn't need a home-field advantage.

My relationship with Junior is a bit complicated. We have some things in common; for example, we both like the Mets and pasta.

Then there are the little glitches, such as my being indirectly responsible for his father's head getting blown off. He's never been thrilled with me about that, although without that little incident he would never have inherited the leadership of the crime family that bears his last name.

But he's calling the shots, so tomorrow night is when we'll be meeting.

The jury will be deliberating by then, if they haven't already come to a conclusion.

There's a little stress in my life right now. I don't think my normal stress-reduction technique, watching football and basketball, is going to do the trick.

I think I'll google *self-induced comas.*

Judge Koenig's charge to the jury is standard, boiler-plate stuff. The only departure from the norm is that he has agreed with Dylan that the jury should be sequestered during their deliberations.

I'm basically okay with that. I opposed it in court mainly because Dylan was in favor of it. I didn't want to spoil my record.

Minutes later the jury is out of the room and deciding how Bobby will spend the rest of his life.

"What do you think?" he asks.

"Whenever a client asks me that, I say I don't know. This time I really don't know. I wish I had something better to tell you."

"You've been through this a lot?"

"Way too many times."

"I don't know how you handle the pressure."

I could tell him that however the jury rules, I will go home to Laurie and Ricky and walk the dogs and live my life. He'll be in a cell and will have an hour a day to exercise in the prison yard.

But I don't say it because he knows it all too well. All I say is, "Good luck."

I spend the rest of the day in what can only be called

a state of double dread. I dread a verdict, because in this case I think that the longer they take, the better. I don't have a reason for that, and I'm sure the negative me will, if they take a long time, decide that's a bad sign.

I'm also dreading in a more immediate sense the meeting with Joseph Russo, Jr., tonight. I instigated it, so I have no one to blame but myself, but that doesn't mean I like the idea.

Laurie, being Laurie, insists that Marcus go with me. I could argue, but I would lose. If I still insisted on going alone, she would handcuff me to the refrigerator, using those handcuffs that I didn't know she kept in the house.

The truth is that I am fine with Marcus going. We'll be in a restaurant, so I have no reason to think that violence will break out, but Marcus makes me feel secure. I'm sure that Laurie and Corey will also be in the area, in case they are needed, but she hasn't mentioned it.

I always have a seemingly unending list of superstitions that I observe while waiting for a verdict, things that I always do and always avoid. I'm breaking one of them tonight: one of the things I always avoid is meeting with the heads of organized crime families.

I asked Marcus to pick me up at eight thirty. He's the most punctual person I know, so at eight twenty-nine I go outside, and he pulls up about thirty seconds later. Twenty-five minutes later we're pulling up to Giarusso's.

I've been through things like this before, including both with Junior and his father, but I'll never get used to it. I'm somewhere between nervous and petrified; Marcus, on the other hand, looks like he is in danger of falling asleep.

We get out of the car and head toward the entrance.

Here goes.

The first thing I realize when we open the door is that the restaurant is closed. So much for being safe because we're in a public place.

I'm not sure why it's closed; it's probably just that Junior decreed it. For all I know, he owns the place.

Russo is sitting at a table, with two of his men on each side of him. Russo is two hundred and thirty pounds, most of it muscle. The other four guys probably go around two-fifty each, also in great shape.

Two empty seats are on the other side of the table. I'm going out on a limb and assuming we're supposed to sit in them. I see a bathroom door off to the side; I hope Clemenza has taped a gun to the toilet.

Russo doesn't say hello; he opens with "I figured you'd bring your friend."

"We're inseparable," I say. "We finish each other's sentences."

Russo turns to one of his men. "If I had this guy, I wouldn't need any of you." Russo has seen Marcus in action before.

"Why are we here?" Russo asks. "You are aware that I don't like you?"

"I have gotten that impression in the past. I was hoping you'd outgrow it."

"What is this information I need to hear?"

"I met with James Pritchett the other day, at his request. I assume you're familiar with him?"

"Keep talking."

"Here is part of what he had to say."

I take my phone out of my pocket and play an edited version of my conversation with Pritchett.

"Richard Minchner was involved in a business relationship with Drew Churasick; I believed . . . I believe . . . they killed Theresa Minardo."

"Why?"

"I'm not sure; understand I was not part of any of these discussions . . . but . . . I think they might have killed Alex Oliva."

"What reason would they have for killing Oliva?"

"It's all about Aaron Widener. He's running for governor. They own him; Widener is in their pocket."

"Who is 'they'?"

"Churasick and Minchner; I don't know who else was involved."

"Jerry Conti ring a bell?"

"I have no firsthand knowledge of that . . . really, I don't."

"What about Joseph Russo?"

"Junior? This much I do know; whoever is behind this will tolerate him for a little while and then send him on his way. Whether he wants to go or not."

"Russo might have a different point of view on that."

"Junior will be in over his head, whoever is behind this. That's for sure."

"Why were all these bombings happening?"

"At one point they were planning those things to make Oliva look bad, but I know they didn't like Womack, the acting mayor. Maybe they wanted to hurt him also."

Russo, while not generally known for his inscrutable poker face, this time does not betray what he's feeling. There is no way he could have heard that and not be pissed off.

"Why was he speaking to you?" Russo says, which is a damn good question, and the first one I asked myself.

"Because when the trial is over, no matter how it comes out, he and Conti think that's it. They don't think the police will still be investigating, but if I lose, they know my team and I won't let it drop. So he's trying to lead us in the wrong direction, to look at the wrong people. But I know better."

"You do?"

I smile with all the fake self-confidence I can muster. "I know everything."

"And what is your reason for coming here?"

"Because I'm going to blow the whole thing up. And if something happened to me, the other members of my team all know about it, and they'll light the fuse. But you can stay clear of it; I just need your help."

"What kind of help?"

"Call Pritchett, tell him the word on the street is that Carpenter is close to figuring it out. That you're not going down, that you'll give up him and Conti before that happens. Tell him he better fix it. Tell him that Carpenter can be bought off."

"That's it?"

"That's it, and it has the advantage of being true."

Russo agrees to go along with it, as I figured he would.

After I finish explaining what I want from him, he agrees to help. There's no downside for him, only upside, especially since his arrangement with Conti is over either way.

"How did you figure it out?" he asks, as Marcus and I are about to leave.

"Hyman Roth."

We're called into court because the jury has a message for the judge.

They did not say they have a question and certainly did not say they have a verdict, so I'm not sure what it is they have to say. I doubt that they want to ask the judge to convey their apologies to Andy Carpenter for putting him through this trial since there is no way his client is guilty.

Every communication between the jury and the judge is done in open court with the lawyers present; there are no secrets here.

My guess is that they are going to say they cannot reach a verdict, and that's what happens. The foreperson says they are deadlocked, with a resolution unlikely.

"Is this on both counts?" Judge Koenig asks.

"Yes, Your Honor."

There is no way that the judge is going to accept this and order a mistrial; the jurors have simply not deliberated long enough. He sends them back to try harder, though taking care to tell them that they should continue to vote their consciences and not acquiesce to the majority simply to achieve unanimity.

In my experience, the judge's sending the jury back usually works, though obviously not always. I have no idea what I want to happen here because I don't know what the current count is.

I'm disappointed that they haven't come to a verdict on the Minardo charge; I think that's one we should win. If they're not giving us that, we may have a problem.

As the court session ends, I see James Pritchett standing in the back, waiting for me. Russo has obviously done his part and made the call.

I take my sweet time about going back there, pretending to be going over paperwork, but really trying to get my nerves under control. I also want the gallery to empty out some more, so that Pritchett and I won't be overheard.

Laurie is across the way on the other side of the gallery, watching, knowing what is going on and getting ready to intervene in the unlikely event that it is necessary.

I finally work my way back there.

Pritchett steps in front of me. "We have to talk."

"All we do is talk. Talking time is over." I'm trying to convey a controlled anger, and I think I'm doing a damn good job of it.

"Whatever your problems are, I can make them right."

"Yeah? Here's my problem. That jury can come in any-time and send my innocent client away for the rest of his life."

Pritchett looks around, to make sure he can't be over-heard. "I told you Churasick killed Oliva and Minardo. I can get you the proof and then your boy goes free and everybody's happy."

"You're still talking. When I have the proof in my hands, then we have something to talk about."

"Give me twenty-four hours."

"It's not my time to give you. When that jury comes in, then it's too late. I break the story, and it's all about you and the two guys above you. And neither of them will let you off the hook, because I'll make sure they know you blew it."

"I'll call you." Pritchett walks off. "Don't do anything until you hear from me."

"And don't call me until you're ready to turn over the proof."

Yesterday was another day without a verdict, and without a phone call from James Pritchett. I am going insane.

I have long ago decided that the deliberations going on this long means bad news for us. I'm now rooting for a hung jury, though that would involve the nightmare of another trial. We know much more now, so we would be a lot better prepared for a retrial than we were for the original. Of course, the same is true for Dylan and the prosecution.

I take the dogs for their morning walk, bringing my cell phone with me. I've carried it for days now, and it never seems to ring.

But when we're on the way home, this time it does: "It's Pritchett."

"Took you long enough."

"I've got what you wanted."

"Proof that I can present to the court?"

"Yes. When can we meet?"

"I have to stay near court today, in case there's a verdict. So it will have to be tonight . . . seven o'clock."

"Where?"

"My office."

"No good. I can't be seen with you or at your office. If certain people knew what I was doing . . ."

"Okay. Eastside Park. At the tennis courts, right near where Oliva's body was left. We'll bring this full circle."

"Okay," he says.

"And come alone."

"I will. And so should you. No one can know what I'm doing."

"I understand."

I hang up the phone and head home as fast as Sebastian's legs will carry him. I have a lot to do.

I update Laurie, and her first question is "So you're going through with this?"

"I am."

"I understand why you're doing it, but it makes me nervous."

"Join the club."

But I can't turn back now. I pick up the phone and call Mayor Oscar Womack's office. He's in a meeting, but I leave word that it is absolutely urgent . . . an actual matter of life and death. I'm not sure I've ever used that phrase before.

But it works; Womack calls me twenty minutes later. "Life and death? What are you talking about?"

"James Pritchett, who worked for Minchner, is meeting me in Eastside Park tonight. He's supposed to be bringing material that could bring down Joseph Russo and Jerry Conti, as well as get my client off the hook. And Aaron Widener is apparently involved."

That obviously got his attention. "I'm listening."

"I think he may try and get out of the bind he's in by killing me. He may have someone with him."

"What the hell are you getting into? This is dangerous stuff."

"That's what I meant by life and death. But I'm defending my client."

"So why are you calling me?"

"I want you to authorize the department to have cops in place before we get there. They can intervene if Pritchett tries anything; otherwise they just stay hidden and I get what I want."

"You're sure about this? I don't want to send cops in and have this turn out to be bullshit."

"I'm sure. I could go to Bauer myself, but he's obviously an Oliva guy, since Oliva made him commissioner. I'm not sure how anxious he would be to send in the cavalry to help Bobby Nash's lawyer."

"Okay, tell me exactly what you want. I'll make sure Bauer does not screw it up."

I tell him the details, and Womack says, "They'll be in place in the park; don't worry about that. Just you be careful."

"I will. Thanks."

Almost as soon as I break off the call, my phone rings again. I see by the caller ID that it's Rita Gordon, the court clerk. That can only mean one thing.

"Come on down, Andy."

"We have a verdict?"

"On one of the counts; they're hung on the other. I don't know which one they've got."

"I'm on my way."

This is shaping up as an eventful day.

Eddie Dowd is already at the defense table when I arrive.

I can see the stress in his face; here's a guy who played in an overtime NFL playoff game, and I'd bet he's never experienced tension like this before.

It's all going to be about which count they've reached a verdict on. If it's the Minardo count, then I think we'll get a not guilty, and the Oliva verdict will be hung. But if it's the Oliva count that they are unanimous on, then it's guilty, Minardo is hung, and we are screwed.

That's the way I am looking at it because I have thought all along that we mounted a better defense on the Minardo homicide. But nothing is less important that what I thought all along, or what I think right now, because the decision has been made, and we're about to find out what it is.

I look across at Dylan and we make eye contact. There's no gamesmanship anymore; we are both scared and worried and tense. We know what the other has gone through. We don't have to like each other, but we are members of a pretty small club.

I look at the gallery and see Laurie, Corey, and Vince Sanders sitting together. Vince looks like a nervous wreck; he should have brought Duchess to calm him down.

Bobby is brought in by the bailiff and sits between Eddie and me. "They won't tell me anything. Is there a verdict?"

"On one count; they are apparently hung on the other."

"Which one do we hope they reached the verdict on?"

I might as well be honest with him. "I'm hoping for Minardo; that's our best shot."

He's about to ask me what the hell this means for us when the judge comes in and gavels open the proceedings. Judge Koenig explains that the jury has sent a message that they have a verdict on one count and are hopelessly deadlocked on the other.

His plan is to call them in, get the verdict on the record, then release them and declare a mistrial on the second count. Before he summons them, he cautions everyone in the court to be quiet and respectful with no outbursts once the verdict is reached.

Judge Koenig asks the bailiff to bring the jury in, and as they file in, three of them look at Bobby and the rest don't. That is either a good sign or a bad sign; I've been doing this for a lot of years, too many years, and I still have no idea.

Judge Koenig confirms with the foreperson that they have reached a verdict on one of the counts, and he asks that the verdict form be handed to the bailiff. The bailiff then brings it to the judge, who looks at it, then gives it back to the bailiff, to give it to the clerk to be read.

The entire process takes about a week and a half, or at least that's how long it seems.

The judge asks Bobby to rise, and Eddie and I do as well. I put my arm on Bobby's shoulder, partly because it's a superstition of mine, and partly to hold myself up. My legs do not seem up to the job.

The court clerk reads it to herself before she's ready to read it out loud. Now it feels like everyone in the United States already knows the verdict except me.

Finally, she begins reading, in slow motion.

"As it relates to count two, the first-degree homicide of Theresa Minardo"—I am so happy to hear the name Theresa Minardo that I almost don't hear the rest—"we, the jury, in the case of the State of New Jersey versus Robert Nash, find the defendant, Robert Nash, not guilty."

I squeeze Bobby's shoulder. This is not a victory; he still stands accused of murder, but it's a hell of a lot better than the alternative. It went as well as it could have gone, considering the circumstances.

Judge Koenig's anti-outburst admonition has proven only partially effective, as there was considerable noise from the gallery when the verdict was read.

He gavels them quiet and releases the jury, thanking them for a job well done. I'm not sure I'd go that far.

I make a motion that Bobby be released on bail, and Judge Koenig says that he will take it under consideration. It would be a gutsy move on his part, but I'm hopeful.

It will now be up to Dylan to decide whether to retry the case. Because of the high profile nature of the case and the victim, there will be a lot of pressure on him to do so.

Judge Koenig adjourns court, and I signal to Vince, who comes over. "Vince, get your reporters on this. I want to find out what the vote was on the Oliva count. The jurors don't have to reveal it, but usually some of them can't resist."

"Okay, I'm on it."

"Good. If it's in our favor, I want to use it to put pressure on Dylan not to retry, or if he does, maybe on the judge to grant bail."

"I'm all over it," Vince says. Then, "You coming to Charlie's tonight? You can buy me a beer."

"Vince, I wish I was, believe me. Unfortunately, I have other plans."

You want me to put that on?" I ask.

Laurie is holding up what I believe is a bullet-proof vest. I have no idea where she got it . . . maybe from her handcuff drawer.

"Yes. Actually, I insist on it."

"It will make me look fat."

"Better than looking dead."

"Laurie, the place will be crawling with cops."

"They will be wearing these things as well. Andy, this is not negotiable."

When Laurie describes something as nonnegotiable, there is no point in negotiating. So I take the vest from her, and with her help I put it on.

"This is not very heavy," I say.

"Five pounds. Small price to pay to save your life."

"What if he shoots me in the head?"

She thinks for a moment. "I would describe that as an insurmountable problem."

I've been a nervous wreck all day, and for some reason wearing the vest increases my panic. Maybe that is because just my wearing it means I'm in serious danger; people don't wear bulletproof vests to the opera, or to their kid's dance recital.

There is always the chance that Pritchett is going to play this straight, that he's going to give me some kind of proof implicating Churasick in the killings, in return for my promise to back off. I'd be shocked if that turns out to be the case, but either way he is not going to leave the park a free man.

The day has gone incredibly slowly, but not as slowly as I'd like. Finally it is six forty-five. I kiss Ricky, pet the dogs, hug Laurie by pulling her close into my bulletproof vest, put my jacket on over the vest, and go out to the car.

The danger, the only significant danger, is that Pritchett will shoot right away, before the cops have a chance to intervene. There is also the chance that the other Conti goon who flew in to New Jersey, who is so far unaccounted for, will elude the police and do the shooting. With all the cops that will be in place, that seems, to use an unfortunate but apt phrase, a long shot.

Laurie doesn't think Pritchett would take the shoot-first approach anyway. She thinks he would want to find out how much I know, and who else knows it. She seems to think he could coerce me into talking by inflicting pain and threatening death. I would say she is right about that.

I drive the short distance to Eastside Park and pull up near the tennis courts. I then walk toward where Oliva's body was found; it's darker there and it's also near the trees where the cops will be in hiding.

Three minutes later a car pulls up and James Pritchett gets out. He sees where I am and starts walking toward me. He's holding what looks like a manila envelope.

"Here you go." He hands me the envelope, which is sealed. "We have a deal?"

I hold up the envelope. "If this has what it's supposed to have, we have a deal."

I start to walk, knowing he won't let me.

"Wait. How do I know you'll back off?"

"I would never lie; I'm a lawyer."

He laughs at that.

"If this gets my client off, that's all I care about."

"I've got something else for you to care about." Suddenly a gun seems to appear in his hand out of nowhere.

"What are you doing?"

"Well, at this point I'm just holding a gun on you. But there's more fun stuff to come. By the way, that envelope is empty."

"Come on, can't you let this go? I'm not going to cause you any problems." I'm trying to sound afraid, which doesn't take De Niro–level acting, since I am afraid. I don't care how many police officers are ready to rush in, something about a gun being pointed at me makes me feel vulnerable.

"Sorry. Can't help you with that."

"So you killed Oliva."

"Not actually me; it was Churasick."

"Why did he have to die?" I know the answer, but I have to hear him say it because I am recording it on my phone.

"Because he wasn't running for governor; he was going to stay as mayor. We couldn't have that."

"And Minardo?"

"She knew too much; Minchner had a big mouth and

told her more than he should have. And killing her made your boy look even more guilty. It was a win-win."

"The police are surrounding you right now. I called Mayor Womack; he authorized the operation."

Pritchett laughs again. "Womack? You really don't know anything, do you? Womack has been what this is about from the beginning. We own Womack. He didn't authorize any cops to come here; he called me instead."

"You're lying."

"Yeah? The only other person here is my man, who's in hiding to deal with anyone else you might have brought with you. But you were so stupid that you came alone." He yells, "Come on out, Hank."

"Freeze, asshole! Drop the gun!"

I'm glad there's enough light that I can see the expression on Pritchett's face when he realizes that isn't Hank talking.

"Playing the role of Hank at this performance is the New Jersey State Police," I say.

Instead of dropping the gun, Pritchett suddenly whirls, as if to fire at wherever the voice came from. I don't know if he is going to shoot or not, or even whether his mind registers that fifteen state cops, including a SWAT team, are facing him.

But he is pointing the gun at them, and that's the only thing they need to know, so they fire.

They kill him and miss me, which is a good thing. I had no interest in testing the vest.

Pete Stanton comes over to me, and Laurie, Corey, and Marcus soon appear out of nowhere. I also see Lieutenant

Briggs of the state police walking toward me. I bought three steaks for him at Charlie's; it was money well spent.

I have just a two-word question for him. "Mayor Womack?"

Briggs nods. "Being arrested as we speak."

J udge Koenig doesn't know much about the events of last night. He's seen the media reports, so he knows that James Pritchett is dead and Acting Mayor Oscar Womack has been arrested and is in custody.

But while the judge doesn't know many of the details, he quickly agreed to this meeting in chambers this morning.

Lieutenant Briggs is here as well, as is Dylan, of course. I don't know how much Dylan knows; he's been fairly quiet, but he's going to be a key player here.

The court reporter has been taking everything down as I have been detailing the conspiracy: "The entire operation was premised on removing Alex Oliva from the mayor's office, by whatever means necessary. The original story that my client wrote, while not technically correct, was handed to him on a silver platter. Minchner and Theresa Minardo orchestrated it."

"In order to get Oliva to resign?" the judge asks.

"No. They knew that once they stepped forward and proved the story wrong, it would actually help him by demonstrating that the media and establishment were against him. They wanted to enhance his chances to become governor; he was already the favorite, even without their help."

"To that extent it worked."

I nod. "It sure did. He became the crusader who would defy the media out to get him. He played it brilliantly. I can't be sure, but I think he, Minchner, and Minardo were all in on it. They knew the story would quickly be disproven, so it wouldn't damage him at all. The opposite would be true.

"But Oliva and Minardo did it so he could become governor. Minchner did it to get rid of him as mayor. Minchner and Conti just wanted Womack to be mayor; that's all they cared about."

"But Oliva was running for governor, and since he was favored to win, why kill him? Hadn't they gotten what they wanted?"

I shake my head. "He had decided against running and was going to stay on as mayor, but hadn't revealed it publicly. His wife told me that he had only told a few select people in city government. One of those would have been Womack, as head of the City Council. Womack then told James Pritchett, and that's why Oliva had to be eliminated."

Dylan asks a question for the first time. "Why was it so important for Womack to be mayor? What would Conti have to gain by that?"

That's been the key question all along. "Did you ever see *Godfather Two*?"

Dylan frowns. "Of course."

"There's a scene in Cuba, and Hyman Roth is talking about how great things are going to be for the crime families. He says something like, 'Here we are, protected, in partnership with a friendly government.'"

"And Womack represented the friendly government?"

I nod. "You know how much Paterson's budget was last year? More than three hundred million. And Passaic County is another four hundred million. Womack was putting all his people in place; he had gotten rid of the planning commissioner and was going to dump the police commissioner and all of Oliva's people.

"We're talking about seven hundred million dollars a year. They could have made fifty million in profit just by corrupt contracts, and it all would have been hidden. It was a cash cow, a license to steal a fortune as long as Womack was in office.

"Had Bobby Nash died in that car, as he was supposed to, they would have gotten away with it. The police would have decided that he was guilty, and that would have been the end of it."

I turn the meeting over to Lieutenant Briggs, who basically confirms all that I've said, adding details. He also describes the events of last night, and how I asked Womack to provide police protection, knowing that he wouldn't, to make James Pritchett feel in control. "Mr. Carpenter then spoke to Captain Stanton, who contacted me, and the state police provided the police presence that Womack did not."

We wrap things up by playing the recording on my phone from last night, which essentially represented a confession by Pritchett that he and his people committed the two murders for which Bobby was charged. It sums things up quite well.

Judge Koenig asks Dylan what he is going to do. It's up to the prosecution to decide whether to retry the case, since the jury had been deadlocked on one of the charges.

"In light of these events and the new evidence," Dylan says, "it seems inconceivable that we can convince a jury of Mr. Nash's guilt beyond a reasonable doubt. And we no longer have an interest in doing that. On a matter with this high a public profile, I will have to consult with the department leadership, but I cannot imagine that we will proceed with this prosecution."

"Thank you," I say. "But we need more than a decision not to retry. We need an affirmative declaration that Mr. Nash is innocent."

Dylan nods. "You'll have it."

Before I even had a chance to plan our traditional victory party, Vince has made all the arrangements.

He's gotten the upstairs private room at Charlie's and sent out invitations. It's a bigger party than usual; in addition to me, Laurie, Corey, Marcus, Sam, Pete, Willie, Sondra, the Bubeleh Brigade, and, of course, Bobby Nash, Vince has invited a bunch of people from the newspaper, including the publisher. Edna couldn't make it; she's on a cruise ship, enjoying a vacation with her fiancé.

The good news is that Bobby is being welcomed back to the paper and will also write a book about his experiences. The word is that they are expecting a bidding war over it.

"This is nice of you to do," I say to Vince. "I assume you're paying?"

"Don't be ridiculous. First of all, I wouldn't insult you; paying the tab at Charlie's is your thing. Second, I've set the whole thing up, without charging a fee. You know what party planners generally get? You owe me one."

I haven't had a chance to talk much with Bobby since the dismissal of the charges, and he has a bunch of questions, mostly concerning how I knew about Pritchett and Womack.

"For one thing, of the three calls that we thought Minchner made to Conti, two were from his office phone, and the other from his cell. It struck me that since Pritchett worked in the office, maybe he was the one who made the calls. I couldn't be sure, obviously, but it got me wondering.

"Then Pritchett warned me after we subpoenaed Minchner that I had better not reveal Minchner's affair with Theresa Minardo. But I hadn't mentioned it to anyone other than Womack, so he had to be the one to have told them that I knew about it.

"I think it was Pritchett who had Theresa killed, not Minchner. Pritchett knew everything Minchner did, so he knew they would be at the Hilton that night. He used the opportunity to send Churasick in to plant the bomb.

"It all seemed to make sense that Pritchett was Conti's guy, and that rather than being Minchner's assistant, he was really in charge. But I couldn't be sure until Pritchett told me that they owned Aaron Widener. I knew he was lying because I knew it was Womack that they owned.

"How did you know that?" Laurie asks, having overheard our conversation.

"Like I said, Womack had to have told Pritchett that I knew about the affair. But more importantly, Womack would have been one of the few people to know that Oliva had decided not to run for governor. And as a top city official, he also would have known the private line in Oliva's house that Bobby supposedly called with those threats.

"It all fit. Womack was bad-mouthing Oliva and replacing all his people. He was building a corrupt government that Conti would own. But even then I wasn't completely positive until Joseph Russo confirmed it."

"Why was Conti coming to Paterson?" Bobby asks.

"It's just the right size; it has a budget big enough to make it very worthwhile and is small enough to control the government. You couldn't pull this off in a city the size of Detroit, or Philly. Also, Joseph Russo was fine with it; he welcomed it."

"Will anything happen to Russo?" Laurie asks.

"No, he's cooperating, so he'll skate. Conti, I'm not so sure, but that will be up to the Feds to put together."

"What about the explosions at the bus station and American Legion Hall?" Bobby asks.

"It was a brilliant stroke. It was designed to make Womack look like the conquering crime fighter; the man in charge, and at the same time give him the opportunity to make Commissioner Bauer look like an ineffectual jerk. What Churasick and Minchner didn't know was that their own deaths would represent the final victory for Womack."

Vince comes over and asks Bobby, "Did you tell them the big news?"

"You mean about me coming back to work?"

"No."

"About me writing a book?"

"No."

A light goes on in Bobby's eyes. "Oh, I know what you mean. I'm letting Vince keep Duchess. She was only with me a few weeks, and she's much more attached to him now."

"Pretty cool, huh?" Vince asks.

"I was thinking maybe I could rescue a dog from your foundation?" Bobby asks.

"Absolutely. Set up a time with Willie to come by."

"Andy, I can never thank you enough," Bobby says.

Vince shakes his head. "Come on, that's what he does. He's a lawyer."

I nod. "It's true. I'm a lawyer."

Vince leans in and talks softly, so that no one can hear. "Andy, thank you. I will never forget this."

"Sure you will. You will absolutely forget it."

He looks puzzled. "Forget what?"